"Are you okay?" Se   across from her.

She weakly nodded. "Just haven't been back to the office since before New Year's. Going to be like starting all over again."

"I am sure they missed you."

"Don't know about that." She searched the house before them. "But now—" Thinking about the girls made her miss them already. "Those girls have become my everything, I guess."

Sean started unloading measuring tools. "It sure makes life full to have kids in your care. The great thing is, the longer you are apart, the sweeter the reunion is. So just be ready for lots of hugs tonight. Lottie probably gives very enthusiastic ones."

"Oh yes, knock-off-your-feet-bulldozing ones." Elisa just shook her head with a fading smile. "I better get going." Her heels clicked as she walked up the pavement to the garage's side door and prepared herself for the coming day. A new normal. She needed to focus on work now.

Although she'd be excited to return and test Sean's theory that her welcome home would make her feel loved and not forgotten.

Texas transplant **Angie Dicken** lives in Iowa with her family of six, balancing a busy schedule of school sports and activities, date nights with her husband and get-togethers with her longtime friends. Setting sweet romance stories in the beloved heartland seems as natural as sweet corn in the summer and snowplows in the thick of winter. Angie is a multi-published author and an ACFW member. Check out her books and news of upcoming releases at www.angiedicken.com.

Books by Angie Dicken

Love Inspired

Once Upon a Farmhouse
His Sweet Surprise
Her Chance at Family

Love Inspired Historical

The Outlaw's Second Chance

Visit the Author Profile page at LoveInspired.com.

Her Chance
at Family

Angie Dicken

LOVE INSPIRED
INSPIRATIONAL ROMANCE

LOVE INSPIRED®
INSPIRATIONAL ROMANCE

Recycling programs for this product may not exist in your area.

ISBN-13: 978-1-335-59863-9

Her Chance at Family

Copyright © 2024 by Angie Dicken

For questions and comments about the quality of this book, please contact us at CustomerService@Harlequin.com.

Love Inspired
22 Adelaide St. West, 41st Floor
Toronto, Ontario M5H 4E3, Canada
www.LoveInspired.com

Printed in U.S.A.

And we know that all things work together
for good to them that love God, to them who are
the called according to his purpose.
—*Romans* 8:28

In loving memory of Lula Karas.
I wish that I could sit with you over coffee
and kourabiethes one more time.
I love you, Yiayia.

Chapter One

Elisa Hartley pulled into the shadowy driveway, admiring the orange sky bleeding through the bare branches of the elm trees lining her back fence. Through her rearview mirror, she spied the two little girls snoozing in her back seat.

This was it. She was doing this. How could the past few months of double-whammy grief bring her back to this house she couldn't wait to get rid of? She ran her hand through her hair and pressed her head back against her seat. A humorless, breathy laugh escaped her throat.

Ironic.

This old Victorian had been purchased to share with someone she loved. Yet she'd never imagined the reality that, instead of her now ex-fiancé, Chad, two small children would live with her, both in desperate need of the security of this old house, and both had captured her heart in a different way.

If only that truth was a salve to her wound. She was trying to see it as such.

But this was a totally different frame of heart for Elisa. Especially since her experience with children had been limited to volunteering at the church nursery once a quarter. Alongside her parents, Elisa had spent every minute this January caring for these two little girls. Lottie and Ava had endured more loss in their young lives than most people endured in their entire lifetimes.

Elisa was exhausted...in more ways than one. Of course, the sleepless nights and roller-coaster days were to be expected from the girls after they'd lost their parents in a car accident on New Year's Eve. The soft breathing of the four-and two-year-old for most of their two-hour drive from Elisa's parents' home in Grangewood was a sweet reprieve from the nightmare that had been the past few weeks.

A movement caught Elisa's eye. She leaned forward, wondering if her own tired mind was playing tricks on her. A loud squeal grated her ears, and she whipped around to check if Lottie and Ava would wake after such an unnerving noise. *Still sound asleep.* The wind must have blown open the rusty wrought iron gate leading to the backyard.

Leaving the car on, she quietly opened her door and stepped onto the pavement. *Wait a minute.* While the lawn was packed with a typical northeastern Iowa helping of snow, the driveway nearly sparkled. There wasn't a speck of snow to be seen. Maybe a neighbor had been kind enough to clear the concrete for her?

But she didn't know any of her new neighbors. She'd spent a few weeks on-site overseeing the interior remodel of the Victorian home for her clients, the Griffins, back in the fall. Elisa had had no idea that they were going to put it on the market right before her project was finished—and she had not expected to spontaneously snatch up the house without consulting her fiancé...ex-fiancé. They'd dreamed of a house in a quiet community with a decent commute for each of them. Rapid Falls seemed perfect, and Elisa had thought the house would be a fun surprise for Chad.

The familiar ache seared her chest—one that usually meant anxiety before a phone call with a difficult client. But now the pressure was a painful reminder that all she'd once hoped for had come crashing down on her wedding day.

Elisa gently closed the car door, letting it rest on the car frame so it wouldn't completely latch and disturb the girls. Her plan to get them out without too much fussing had not fully formed in her new-guardian brain. First, she'd take care of that gate—

"Hey, there." A deep voice materialized into a tall figure from the shadowy fence line, sending Elisa's entire frame into a rigid ready-to-flee mode as she reached for the handle of the car. "Didn't want to startle you."

Too bad, bud, you already did.

The man stepped into the fading wintry light. Twilight glinted off his wire-framed spectacles. His lips parted as if he were going to speak, but he didn't. He just stared at her.

Elisa took a step back, balling her hands into fists by her side. "Can I help you?"

He pushed back the fur-lined hood of his winter coat. His sandy brown hair stuck up in a boyish mess, and a five-o'clock shadow dusted his strong jaw. "You're the owner here?"

Did his voice just crack? Why did he appear so surprised?

"I am. And you are?"

His mouth remained open, as if whatever words were going to come out froze before they sounded. He then licked his lips quickly and said, "Oh, sorry. I am Sean Peters." He hesitated, wiping his hand on the side of his coveralls but not extending it for a handshake. "The Griffins told me that you would get in touch about the backyard. They hired me."

"Ah, you're the landscape architect." Relief coursed through Elisa's shoulders. He wasn't some creepy stranger hiding out on her property. "I'm Elisa Hartley. So, have you been waiting here all winter?" She teasingly smirked, then crossed her arms over her coat, mostly in an attempt not to shiver. Her car thermometer had read a whopping eight degrees when she pulled into Rapid Falls.

"Us landscape guys specialize in snow removal during these slow business months. I thought I'd clear your driveway for you." He grinned, reaching out to tap the top of a snowblower hiding in the shadow of the garage.

"That's nice of you. How did you know I was coming home?"

Sean stepped closer. "I didn't." His chuckle was warm like hot cocoa, doing the trick in this frigid tundra. "Been helping out most of the senior citizens around here. I noticed your fixer-upper dream house had been sitting dark and alone all of December and January. Better to stay on top of the rising snow inches."

Elisa stiffened. Fixer-upper? Yes. But the dream was long gone. "Well, thank you, Sean. I better get the little ones inside before my car heater succumbs to this cold."

"Little ones? I thought—" His teeth rested on his lips, and he dropped his gaze.

Elisa plastered on a grin, refusing to feel obligated to explain. Obviously, the Griffins had mentioned her soon-to-be newlywed status when they'd told Sean she would be in touch. They had no idea that her status changed from bride-to-be to being the sole guardian of small children.

"They are my nieces." She walked backward to the car, lifting her hand in a wave. Then she quickly yanked the door open and situated herself behind it. "Thanks again."

He nodded and pulled his hood back on. Quickly, he steered the snowblower down the driveway. Elisa lowered into her seat and watched him load it up into a pickup parked along the curb.

"Auntie, are we there yet?" Lottie's sleepy voice cut through the tension in Elisa's shoulders with its sugary sweetness.

"We are, Lottie." She turned and patted the four-year-old's knee. "Just have to pull into the garage." She put the car in Drive and pressed the garage door opener.

In the back corner of the dank space of the garage, totes with Christmas decorations were stacked, untouched, without purpose now that the season was over. Everything would be thick with dust inside the house, and she feared it might take some time to heat the place up.

While Rapid Falls had been working to remove the blanket of ever-present snow over the past two months, Elisa had been shoveling through the remains of her obliterated heart. Not only had her wedding been an unmitigated disaster, but her estranged half brother and his wife—Lottie and Ava's parents—were gone now.

The empty house, bitter winter cold and unfinished projects eerily resembled her life in recent months—unfulfilled and almost forgotten. Elisa had to hope that life in Rapid Falls would be a fresh start. She just needed to rediscover her confidence…if not for herself, then for Lottie and Ava.

The lump in Sean's throat expanded like a snowball rolling down a hill as he climbed into his truck. He couldn't believe that the woman Chad had jilted was the newest Rapid Falls resident. Elisa obviously hadn't recognized Sean, and after witnessing her devastation on her wedding day, he wasn't about to remind her who he was. He'd grown out a beard last fall, and the most they'd seen each other that day was through the rearview mirror of his dad's Mustang. When Sean had received Chad's group text to the college friends that he'd missed his already-delayed flight and taken it as fate, Sean had scrambled from his seat to tell the groomsmen before they began down the aisle. Instead of driving the new-lyweds to the reception, Sean's main task had been to drive the bride away from the church before her guests bombarded her with questions.

How could his old college friend Chad have turned out to be such a heartless guy? They'd lost touch since graduation when Chad had taken a marketing job that sent him all over the country. The first time they'd communicated since then was when Chad asked to use Dad's Mustang for the wedding. And to think Sean had been excited that Chad and his new bride were considering Rapid Falls as a place for their first home. Chad had never told him that a house was bought already.

Something didn't add up.

At least it seemed Elisa was moving forward. And from what the Griffins told him, her upgrades to the interior were outstanding.

The drive home was quick. Sean only lived three blocks away from the Victorian on Birch Street. As he avoided an exceptionally large icy patch near the end of his driveway, he couldn't help but pray for the usual melt into spring to come quickly. That Victorian was going to be his chance to add a design department to the Peters Landscaping business. He laughed at himself. Who was he kidding? He was the design department. And the installation department. And the project manager. But Dad's legacy would be a distant memory if Sean couldn't amp up business in this iffy economy.

Sean had barely used his degree in landscape architecture in recent years. Instead, he'd worked alongside his father's seasonal employees to aestheticize the Rapid Falls commercial district with landscape installation and maintain the yards of loyal customers. But now, in order to thrive, their scope would need to broaden from planting to planning.

If he could gain attention during the Northern Iowa Tour of Remodeled Homes with a restoration of the overgrown backyard at that old Victorian, he hoped to drum up larger projects—design-heavy projects. That was his true talent after all. He'd just tucked it away while assisting his father and helping raise his sister.

Sean stored the snowblower in the shed, then stomped up the deck stairs to the back door of their two-story Craftsman-style home, trying to knock off any remaining snow from his boots. As he unlaced and removed his boots, the bite of the single-digit night air on his damp socks had him hurry into the mudroom. The scent of freshly baked chocolate chip cookies warmed him almost instantly.

"Sean? Is that you?" Blythe's voice was hitched.

"Of course."

His sister still didn't love being home alone. Even if she was a middle schooler now. Thirteen seemed like yesterday for Sean. Maybe because that was his age when Blythe was born. And two years later, he'd become a co-parent with his dad. Sean put his boots on the boot warmer, then stepped out of his lined coveralls and hung them on a hook.

Blythe sat on the bar stool at the kitchen counter with an open textbook and a notebook. "I wish the heater wouldn't make so much noise. It freaks me out." She kept her attention on her homework.

Sean squeezed her shoulder. "I'm always a phone call away—and about a two-second drive." He walked over to a cooling rack of neat rows of golden cookies. "I see you managed your nerves in the very best way."

"Yeah, and also procrastinating seventh grade math."

Sean carefully grabbed a cookie, then headed to the other side of the counter, checking out her work upside down. "Hmm, do you need help?"

Blythe set her pencil down. "No, I get it. But I'd rather bake than crunch numbers." She closed her book. "All done."

"You know, if you want to come help with shoveling, you can. Might be better than being home alone so much."

Blythe plastered a fake smile, braces showing but no hint of glee in her blue eyes. "Oh yippee, manual labor. I'd rather be scared."

Sean chuckled and bit into the cookie, enjoying the melting chocolate and hint of cinnamon. Blythe's personality had blossomed. Dad had pointed it out when Blythe invited a few girls over for her twelfth birthday. She was becoming a young lady. Someone who could joke on a level that was less about knock-knocks and cartoon characters, and more in the form of humorous remarks laced in an everyday conversation.

A twist in Sean's gut made him set the cookie down. It wasn't fair that Dad would miss out on his daughter's journey to adulthood. The cancer had been sudden. Dad had been the one who'd provided stability and a chance for Blythe to grow up in a somewhat steady household. It had all fallen on Dad after their mom left them to fend for themselves.

Sean took a deep breath and tamped down the frustration of their situation. Blythe headed to the living room, turned on the TV and snuggled under an old quilt.

"Want to watch a show?" she asked. "I didn't turn the TV on while you were gone, in case I wouldn't be able to hear a scary sound."

"Well, that doesn't make sense." Sean plopped

down in the recliner and picked up his book from the side table.

Blythe turned toward him. "Yes, it does. What if it was bad enough that I needed to call you? Wanted to be prepared."

"Ah, I see. So, what do you do when I am gone? Sit here with the phone positioned just right, waiting for something bad to happen?" He tossed a throw pillow at her.

"Hey!" She giggled. "I'm not quite that bad. But…just try to be home before dark next time."

"Got it. I will. Sorry, I got carried away at the house on Birch. After I cleared the driveway, I walked around the backyard and tried to get a feel for the place."

"Kinda hard with the snow. That place seems abandoned. Are you sure you'll still get to work on it?"

"I better. I have pretty expensive flagstone piled up at the warehouse. Actually, the owner pulled up when I was leaving." He refrained from sharing with Blythe that he was at the lady's wedding. He hadn't recognized Elisa at first. Gone were her curls and striking makeup from her wedding day. Her straight blond bangs swept across her forehead and were tucked beneath a knit winter hat. Only thick lashes, no eyeliner, accentuated the light brown hue of her eyes— first narrowed in question. But once Sean had introduced himself, Elisa's expression softened, like a brightening sky after a storm. He could only imagine she did not want one more person bringing up her wedding day, and he wasn't going to risk adding any weirdness to their professional relationship. "I had a chance to introduce myself."

"Oh, that's good."

"I think I startled her."

"You can't go around scaring people, Sean. It's not very nice." She tossed the pillow back at him.

"Ha ha, sis. You really are safe here in Rapid Falls. You should know. You've been here all your life."

"But do you watch TV at all? True crime shows or the news?" She pulled the blanket up to her chin. "Scary stuff happens all the time."

Sean leaned over and flipped the channel from a real crime series to a baking show. "Maybe you shouldn't watch that stuff. Keep up the baking, Blythe." He opened his book, his mind far from the words on the page.

This small town and old house had been a constant in their lives. Neither of the Peters kids had lived outside of Rapid Falls, Iowa, except when Sean was at college in Ames. But despite the settled feeling of being home, they'd also gone through enough in their lives for the place to trigger a sense of loss and insecurity.

A sense of being alone and in the dark.

Sean understood her feelings. He recalled the loneliness and sense of abandonment when he was just Blythe's age. And it had nothing to do with monsters or criminals. Just a mother who didn't love them enough to stay.

Chapter Two

The first night at the house was not ideal. After an hour of trying to heat up the place while eating takeout and battling a two-year-old determined to climb the dangerous stairs, Elisa finally made a fire in the living room fireplace. She then laid out blankets on the soft rug she'd purchased to complement the porcelain-white walls. Everything contrasted nicely with the original wood trim and mantel. Her new place had hardly been admired by anyone over the age of five, though.

As they made their pallet, Lottie insisted, "It's a giant nest!"

She quickly piled up throw pillows from the sectional couch, along with the feathered bed pillows Elisa had brought down from upstairs. All the while, little Ava followed her big sister from couch to blankets and squealed and patted the cushions.

"Okay, my little birds," Elisa whispered as she slipped under the comforter, forfeiting her usual nighttime reading habit. "Let's snuggle together. Tomorrow, we'll sleep upstairs." They finally settled down and cuddled close, trying to keep warm.

But for Elisa, the freezing tip of her nose wasn't the only thing that kept her from sleeping. Last time she was in this house, she'd planned a whole life for herself. The bedroom upstairs to the right was going to be her home office, but later—not too much later—she would convert it to a nursery. And the room between the master bedroom would be a guest room and Chad's study. Thankfully, she hadn't wasted her money on the custom-built shelving she'd received a quote for from the local carpentry place.

This house was not letting her go as quickly as her groom had. The moment Elisa decided to put her dream home back on the market, after a month of grieving what would never be, her family's life had turned upside down.

She wrapped the girls with a gentle squeeze of her arm. Two-year-old Ava was tucked between her big sister and her aunt. How could Elisa not hold on to this place a little longer? Her loft in Marion was too small to raise kids. If these girls were going to be in her life for the long term, she may as well have them grow up in a real-life dollhouse.

Ah, that was a good analogy.

She needed to replace dream house with dollhouse. An easy task, in theory. If only the dolls weren't broken on the inside. All three of them.

February passed by in a flurry of babyproofing the house and keeping the girls entertained. Elisa woke up most mornings to Ava shaking the pack-n-play next to Elisa's bed and a dozing Lottie pressed up against her after whimpering on and off all night. The first day of March was much like their first day in Rapid Falls. Several inches of snow outside and couch pillows strewn across the floor downstairs. Elisa and the girls headed upstairs while she tried picturing how she would convert her office and the guest room into bedrooms fit for two princesses.

"It's been tricky, Mom, that's all I have to say," she said to the girls' grandmother on the phone. Ava was on Elisa's hip, trying to squirm her way to the floor.

"Oh, honey, I am so sorry we haven't made it up to help you all get settled. Dad's office has been short-staffed."

"I know, Mom. It's good that the girls and I are figuring this out together…right?" She shifted Ava to her other hip.

"You keep an eye on us, Auntie?" Lottie questioned from the swivel chair at the giant desk. Her crayons were scattered across the shiny finish, surrounding a coloring book.

"What's that, Lottie?" Elisa asked, lowering Ava to the floor and then making a beeline to the door so the two-year-old wouldn't escape. Even though Elisa had double-checked the security of the newly installed baby gate at the top of the stairs, she'd rather Ava stay in the same room as her for good measure.

"You keep an eye on *us* and get off your phone." Lottie continued to color after dishing out a matter-of-fact reprimand. Elisa bit the bottom of her lip, unsure how to respond to that. She finished up her conversation quickly.

"Mom, I'm going to let you go. Let me know when you figure out a weekend to come visit."

"I can't wait. Give the girls kisses from me."

"Okay. Love you. Bye."

"Bye, sweetie."

"I want my sippy." Ava's tiny voice didn't match her larger-than-life energy. She toddled over to the door and smacked her hand just beneath the door handle. "I want my sippy. I want my sippy," she chanted.

"Okay, okay." Elisa sighed and picked her up again, nuzzling her neck as the little girl giggled. "Let's go get that sippy."

"Wait!" Lottie cried out. "Don't leave me." She scrambled down the chair and ran around the desk. She wiped her eyes with the backs of her hands, and her thick brown bangs swept across a furrowed brow.

"Don't worry, Lottie. We'll all go together." The girl did not like being alone. Elisa couldn't blame her.

Lottie clasped her fingers together and tucked them under her chin. "Okay." Elisa placed a hand on her niece's back, and they all maneuvered the stairs slowly, together.

A knock sounded on the front door across from the bottom stair. A figure could be seen in the bright mottled sidelight.

"Dada!" Ava began to squirm from Elisa's arms.

"No, sweetie. No, no." An instantaneous lump lodged in Elisa's throat, and she peered down at Lottie. The young girl looked up and shook her head, then leaned against Elisa's leg with a slumped shoulder. Elisa didn't know how to respond when Ava mentioned her parents. "Let's go see who it is." Elisa readjusted Ava on her hip and opened the door.

Sean Peters stood there wearing the exact same coveralls and fur-lined hood from their first night. "Hey, Elisa. Just wondering if you need me to get your driveway again. I was just finishing up Marge's next door."

Elisa poked her head out the door and looked at the smooth glistening surface of snow. "Oh, wow. We haven't left the house lately."

"Cold!" Ava yelped.

Elisa stepped back inside. "If you have time, that would be great. I was kinda hoping it would all melt away by this time. It's March."

Sean shook his head and quirked an eyebrow. "Where'd you move from again?"

"We came up from Grangewood—a small town near Des Moines—where my parents live."

"Rapid Falls always seems to manage a little longer winter. Funny how we're in a whole different world up here."

"A different world?" Lottie's large brown eyes widened.

Sean chuckled and bent over with his hands on his knees to address Lottie. "That's just an expression. It's different than central Iowa, that's all. Same world."

"Cold!" Ava began to kick her legs.

Sean popped up. "Oh, sorry. I'll not keep you all with the door wide open."

"You want to see our map?" Lottie offered. "Come on, it's in our playroom."

"Oh, that's okay, let Mr. Peters get to work." As the words left her mouth, Elisa felt heat rise in her cheeks. As if this man was an employee. He was a random stranger who happened to be a consultant for a project that would never be. "I mean, not to work for us, but just, just the work of shoveling snow. Thank you so much for the offer, Sean." Elisa tried to close the door.

"Please." Lottie tugged at Elisa's elbow. "Nobody has seen our playroom yet."

Sean boomeranged a look at Lottie then back to Elisa. With a surrendering smile, he said, "I have all the time in the world. The landscaping business is pretty slow this time of year."

Elisa blew out an uneasy breath. "Uh, okay. But excuse the mess. We are still figuring all this out." She hadn't had an adult this close in her proximity since the last time she'd seen Sean. Unless a delivery boy, or three, counted. But this conversation today had lasted much longer than any food order.

"I am impressed with the updates." Sean gazed at the main living room as he slipped off his snow boots and unzipped his coat.

"Pardon the piles of laundry and the pillow fort." Elisa grabbed some folded clothes off the back of the couch and tossed them in the wicker basket at the bottom of the stairs.

"Seriously, though. I've been inside plenty of these historic homes over the years. My dad was friends with many of your neighbors. Most still have decades-old wallpaper and outdated carpet covering the original hardwoods." He ran his hand along the banister. "This house seems right out of a home restoration magazine."

Did this man have an appreciation for design? She tried to brush off the compliment. But how long had it been since she'd felt appreciated? "Thanks. I am still trying to figure out how to do the chores, work on my own projects and keep these two safe and entertained."

She led the way across the living room, lowering Ava to the floor. The toddler took off running toward a set of double pocket doors with glass pane inserts. Lottie ran over and grunted as she pushed on the panels, and with a squeal, the doors slid open to the four-season room.

A dollhouse, several dolls, a few balls and a couple of plastic totes filled with various toys gave away that this was, indeed, the playroom.

"Here, mister—" Lottie held a toy globe the size of her torso.

"Mr. Peters," Elisa corrected.

"Nah, just call me Sean." He crouched down across from Lottie. "What's your name?"

"Lottie Hartley." She pushed the globe to him. "Here's my map."

"Ah, this is a kind of map. It's called a globe, Lottie." He spun the globe around. Lottie's little eyebrows arched into her brunette bangs. "Do you know where Iowa is?"

Elisa nudged Lottie's foot with her own. "Remember, I showed you. The red dot."

"Oh, yeah." Her little hands pushed the globe around as she searched the plastic surface. "Here!"

"Yes, you are right." Sean handed it back. "That's a great toy."

"Globe, you mean?" Lottie pushed a fist on her hip as if she were offended by his choice of words. Elisa made a mental note to talk to the spunky four-year-old about manners when they found some sort of norm.

"Yes, of course." Sean chuckled. Lottie joined Ava at the dollhouse. Sean crossed over to the large floor-to-ceiling windows and examined the backyard. The snow hid all the brambles and the old patio. The only thing that appeared alive were the snowmen Elisa had built with the girls. "Such a great space," he muttered, then turned around. He was a handsome guy. His hazel eyes gleamed with kindness behind his spectacles, and he held his mouth in a relaxed grin. If comfort was personified in a stranger, then Elisa found Sean Peters to be exactly that. A familiar, comforting countenance.

Elisa realized she was lost in thought and shook her head discreetly, deciding it was time to see Sean out of the house. Although, it was nice having another adult around. Even if she would eventually have to let him down professionally.

"So, they are your nieces, right?" Sean crossed the space again. Elisa nodded. "Your neighbor, Marge, said she was thrilled by the family of snowmen in the back. Expect some delicious baked goods coming your way as soon as it warms up. How long are the girls visiting for?"

"Um, I am actually their new guardian." She pulled her long hair back into a ponytail, then spoke low and away from little ears. "Very un-expected."

Sean blew out a long breath and leaned against the opposite doorjamb. They watched the girls play for a moment. "I remember the basement at home when my younger sister went through her doll phase. Every nook and cranny was set up as some sort of pretend room for babies." He pushed his glasses up his nose and shook his head as if he was smack-dab in the middle of memory lane.

Elisa opened her mouth, prepared to speak to Sean about canceling the landscape work, then pressed her lips shut again. She was about to tell this stranger that the backyard was going to be her ex's space but everything had changed. Elisa didn't want to mention her ex at all. Rapid Falls was a fresh start, hours away from the pity looks and quiet whispers about her no-show groom.

She was thankful that nobody knew her around here. Even if the Griffins mentioned a couple would hire him, the only explanation she owed Sean was that she no longer needed his landscape service. May as well be up front with him now.

Sean hooked his thumbs on his coverall suspenders. "Well, I better—"

The coffeepot beeped from the kitchen. "Would you like a to-go cup of coffee to keep you warm out there?" Coffee was a great consolation for bad news.

"Sure. Sounds great." Sean pushed off the doorjamb.

"Lottie, don't let Ava leave the room. I'll be right back," Elisa said.

"Okay. I'm the best helper," Lottie exclaimed, patting her sister on the head between her tiny pigtails.

"You sure are." Elisa pulled at the two sliding doors and closed them. "Luckily, these things squeal when they open. Before, I would have tried to fix them, but now it's my alarm for baby-on-the-loose."

Sean laughed and followed her to the kitchen. Elisa pulled out a disposable coffee cup for Sean and a mug for herself.

"This kitchen is amazing. I love the quartz and copper together." He inspected the countertops.

"You sure know your interior elements. I thought you were Mr. Landscape?"

"Hey, I know good design when I see it." Sean scanned the white cabinets that stretched to the ceiling. He then walked over and ran his hand along the butcher-block island. "It took me a good long while to decide between architecture and landscape architecture. I still subscribe to *Architectural Digest*."

"Well, I appreciate your enthusiasm. I had fun figuring out the look of the place." She handed him the cup and they crossed back toward the four-season room. A brochure fluttered to the floor as they passed the kitchen table. Sean picked it up and flipped through it. Elisa's face heated. The firm had highlighted *"Projects by Elisa Hartley"* for a home expo, and had sent her one to review.

"Wow, Elisa, your work is amazing," he said as he read and sipped his coffee. His gaze glimmered her way. "You are really good at what you do."

"Thanks." She caught a glimpse of her neighbor, bundled in snow gear, walking through the side yard. She changed the subject happily. "It seems like Rapid Falls is a pretty small town."

"You think?" He smiled. "But it's not so small that your business is everyone's. Promise." Sean seemed authentic. Actually, he was genuine. She recalled the Griffins raving about his down-to-earth demeanor. They'd sold her on keeping him on to design Chad's dream backyard. Elisa inwardly shuddered.

A crash sounded from the playroom. "Uh, better check on them. Two minutes is about all I've been able to manage for me-time these past few weeks."

She hurried past him. The sound of little voices seeped through the spacing of the double doors. "Everything okay?" She slid the doors open. The girls were standing over a pile of blocks.

"Ava knocked down my tower." Lottie began to move all the blocks away from her sister.

"Argh. Me a dinosaur!" Ava raised her fists, tightened them and growled so loud her two little pigtails of curls shook.

"Stop!" Lottie stomped her foot.

"You mean." Ava pouted and then toddled over to a bin and began to dig through the toys.

"Girls, remember, we take care of each other," Elisa reminded them with her usual advice for their little squabbles.

"I guess I'd better get to it." Sean sipped his coffee, then set it on the console behind the couch, seemingly taking care to place it on the runner and not the polished wood. He began to pull on his boots in the foyer.

Elisa headed to the door and swiveled around

before opening it to the biting cold. "My plans have changed big-time." She glanced over his shoulder, eyeing her two nieces. "A sophisticated backyard is at the bottom of my list right now. I am sorry, Sean. But the project's off."

Sean just stared at her, as if he were processing her words at half speed. "I understand that plans change. And raising two children…wow." His eyebrows arched above the round rims of his glasses. "I'll give you some time—"

Elisa stopped him. "I am sorry. There really is no reason to move forward." She looked back at the girls, who began to sing the alphabet together. "Those two lost their parents over New Year's. They are all I care to commit to right now. Your favor of clearing our drive is much appreciated, but I won't be remodeling the backyard anytime soon."

"Don't even worry about it." Sean finished tying his laces. "And just so you know, Elisa. I would have cleared your driveway regardless of your client status. But spring's around the corner. Supposed to have the 'Great Thaw' in the next week or so." He winked. "I think you'll see that a new backyard might be just what your new family needs."

She opened the door and he stepped into the bright day, his boots crunching on the packed snowy sidewalk. He disappeared around the corner of the house. Sean Peters was right about one thing. Spring was around the corner. A new season would benefit them all. But he was mistaken if he thought the high-end terraced backyard for entertaining company parties was anything she cared about anymore.

That plan had been for Chad.

Now? She couldn't care less.

Sean pushed the rumbling snowblower down and back, wondering if he'd hoped for too much with this project. Elisa had reluctantly shared her situation, mostly to inform him that he shouldn't count on her business. This wasn't the first time he'd had a client back out when they'd had a whole winter to consider...but he'd never quite had a client whose entire life changed over the course of a Christmas break. How could he convince her to go ahead with the project?

Peters Landscaping needed something more than a few lawns to care for this summer.

Every turn Sean took toward the wrought iron fence, he imagined the delicious aroma rising from that future outdoor fireplace he'd planned to install with the intention to appeal to newlywed professionals needing to relax in the evenings.

What could have been so important to Chad that he'd not even called off the wedding until the very day? Sean had no idea. Maybe that decision had been a sign that Chad's commitment had waned. If they'd kept in touch over the years, Sean might have noticed any red flags long before the wedding, and he could have given Chad some advice. Afterall, Sean understood the risks that went along with any relationship. Would he have held on to his last relationship as long as he had if he had known how attached Blythe would grow to his ex?

Sean was living the perfectly single dream—trying to maintain business for his piece of Rapid Falls commerce and raising his teen sister. He didn't want to risk the heartbreak for himself or for Blythe again. They had lost enough. He let the snowblower idle when he noticed Blythe walking home from school down the street. *Dream or duty?* At least he wasn't like his mother, who chose to chase a dream, leaving loved ones knocked over in her wake. Now Mom kept in touch so infrequently, Sean wasn't sure if it would be better for Blythe to not hear from her at all.

"Hey, peanut," he shouted as he powered down the snowblower.

Blythe waved, then marched faster through the snow in her hot-pink snow pants, purple winter coat and mint-green mittens. About as colorful as her creative personality.

"I am almost done here." He rolled the snow-blower to his truck, lifted it into the bed with a huff and grabbed a shovel. Blythe tossed her backpack in the back seat. "How was school?"

"Okay. I got an A on my math quiz." She wagged her eyebrows with pride.

"Good job. How about we celebrate at the diner for an early dinner?"

Blythe pushed the gathered snow along the rim of his truck bed. "I have that babysitting course at the community center, remember?"

He slung the shovel over his shoulder. "Oh, do I have time to finish the driveway?"

"It's at four."

"Okay. Real quick. This should be the last of my shoveling days this year. Supposed to warm up over the next week. We'll probably see bare ground by Saturday."

Blythe leaned over and grabbed another shovel. "I'll help. Maybe you could get me a snack…like a hot chocolate from Sweet Lula's?"

"Ah, are you striking a deal with me?" Sean struck the pavement with the shovel and slid it under the icy snow.

"Until I start getting paid for babysitting, you'll have to foot my chocolate bill," she snickered.

"You know, there are two little girls that live here. Maybe you can strike a deal with their aunt—babysitting for a landscape project?"

"Um, that seems like she'd be paying two bills. Not much of a deal."

"Huh, they are teaching you something in math class." He flicked a little snow at her.

"Hey, you know I'll win a snowball fight," she warned.

"Only because I let you." He hefted a giant pile of snow and flung it into the yard.

"But seriously, there are kids at this house?"

"Sure are. Two sisters. Not even school age, I'd guess." He studied the living room window.

"Maybe I'll introduce myself once I pass the babysitting class," Blythe suggested. "Would be an easy walk from home." She shoveled and grunted as she added to the snowy yard. "As long as I don't have to watch them at night." She tilted her head back as she studied the pointed gables and decorative trim. "I don't think I'd enjoy all the noises that place probably makes."

"I have a feeling the two little girls would be loud enough. You won't hear a thing."

Blythe tilted her head and gawked at him. "Exactly! I wouldn't be prepared at all."

Sean laughed and tousled her Rapid Falls Eagles knit cap. A movement caught his attention from the corner of his eye.

Lottie Hartley was pressed up against the window, flanked by the white drapes.

"I think we have a spy." Sean spoke quietly to

Blythe, using his eyes to point out the little girl with her nose like a pig snout against the glass.

Blythe ogled in the house's direction. "Aw, she's cute." She waved her bright mittens. The drapes swooshed shut, and Lottie disappeared.

"She's super cute. So is her little sister."

Blythe cooed. "Let's get going so I can get to my class...*after* hot chocolate, of course."

They both continued with the final swath of white stuff the blower had missed. Sean used the rhythmic scooping as thinking time and pondered his original question. How could he persuade Elisa to continue with the project?

Chapter Three

The next week, every resident in Rapid Falls seemed to be out for a walk or cleaning up the soupy mess of slush and grime in their garages. Typical Iowan spring cleaning. Sean was glad to see the patches of dormant grass in the yard— an easy prediction when he saw the forecast. Of course, there was still a bunch of snow, especially piled high at the end of the dead-end street. Kids were climbing the gray-tinted pile now. But unlike two weeks ago, when the weather called for wearing several layers beneath a snowsuit, the kids wore only sweatshirts and jeans. A balmy forty degrees was like a heat wave after a solid month of temps barely reaching the teens.

Sean finished up in his garage and strode to his truck. As he rounded the truck bed, a curdled scream stopped him in his tracks. Lottie Hartley sprinted down the sidewalk, her knit cap's bobble bouncing as she flapped her arms at her side. Close behind the wild girl was Elisa Hartley, pushing a stroller. Giggles poured from the strapped-in two-year-old.

"Lottie, you stop right this instant."

"I'm going home!"

Sean jogged to the end of his driveway and placed his hands on his knees, pushing up his glasses as he steeled himself square on at the oncoming child.

"Hey, mister, move out of the way." Lottie waved her hands at him.

"I think your aunt wants you to slow down."

"I gotta go home." As Lottie slowed and drew near, Sean noticed her tear-streaked cheeks. Maybe from the cold as she ran, but by the wobbling chin, he knew she was probably upset. "I got to get my swing set."

Sean cocked his head. "I don't think a girl as small as you could carry a whole swing set." She was now in front of him with her arms across her worn winter coat.

Lottie pouted. "But I got to get it, mister. My daddy made it for me." That chin began to quiver more fiercely than before.

Elisa stopped the stroller beside them. "Lottie, you can't just—"

Sean stood and held up a hand signaling Elisa

to stop. She gawked at him. "Lottie wants her playset from home."

Elisa swiped off her own knit cap, releasing a long wave of caramel and gold tresses over her shoulder. "I know. And I told her it has new owners now." She slid her hand through her dark blond hair. "We can find a park instead."

Lottie stomped angrily, but then her shoulders shook as she wept into the collar of her coat.

Elisa blanched and stepped around the stroller, crouching next to Lottie. She glanced up at Sean with a look of helplessness.

He bent down again and hooked the little girl's chin. "Hey, there, Lottie. Are you sad because your daddy made the playset for you, like you just told me?"

Elisa's face flushed, and she immediately clutched Lottie against her. "Is that true, Lottie? You should have told me—" The little girl turned and wrapped her arms around Elisa's neck, burying her face in her aunt's long locks. She mouthed to Sean, "I had no idea. It's gone."

Sean didn't know anything about this family. But he knew a thing or two about mourning those who disappeared without warning. He placed his hand on Lottie's back. She pressed back and looked over her shoulder at him. "Mister, could my playset fit in your truck?"

"Uh, well…" Sean rubbed his jaw and absorbed Elisa's intense umber glare. "I don't think we can get it now. But…you know, I helped build the one at the city park. It's a fine playground." Sean's first design project was a charitable contribution during the 150th year of Rapid Falls about five years ago. Since then, he had barely designed anything. Planting annuals in existing flower beds around town, like at the local bank and retirement center, residential lawn maintenance, and keeping up with the seasonal planters along Main Street hardly needed a designer's touch. That could all change. He could make something more happen—if this woman would follow through with their autumn plans.

Lottie wiped her cheeks with each palm. "You build playsets? You build me one!"

Little Ava kicked her legs and grabbed at Lottie. "Me, too!"

"You know, Elisa, I can get equipment at wholesale—"

But Elisa was more focused on the excited children. "Not now, girls." Elisa grabbed Lottie's hand. "Sean, where's that city park you mentioned?" She crammed her hat back on her head, pushing long wisps of hair to the corners of her eyes.

"Uh, I don't know if you heard me say…" Sean swallowed hard, debating whether he should really mention this now. "If you follow through with the plan, we can find a way to fit a—" He turned his head away so the girls couldn't see him spell, "P-l-a-y-s-e-t."

Elisa glared at him in such a way that he immediately regretted his course of action. This was not a good idea after all. She strode over so she was directly in front of him with her back to the girls. She was only a few inches shorter than him. From the corner of her pursed mouth she whispered, "This is really none of your concern."

"Actually, it kind of is." Sean shrugged his shoulders to his ears and pushed his glasses up. "My company really counted on this project."

"And that's not really my concern." She spun around so fast he caught a giant whiff of blossoms and a hint of citrus. She yanked the stroller handle and secured Lottie's hand in hers once again.

"Please, Elisa—we need to talk about this—" But as he tried to find words that wouldn't make him sound completely insensitive to her situation, the storming woman whipped that stroller so quickly that Sean decided it was best to just keep his mouth shut. However, if Peters Landscaping's books were correct, inflation had taken a toll. After the expenses for Dad's hospital bills and funeral costs, Sean was uneasy about the future of the family business.

* * *

Elisa wasn't sure if she was more upset that the guy was trying to use her niece's situation to secure a business deal, or that he had taken the time to understand Lottie's desperation for her playset when Elisa had assumed the girl was overreacting.

"Lottie, did your daddy really build a whole playset?"

Lottie pulled her sleeve along her nose and sniffled. "Uh-huh. He let me help paint it."

"That's pretty special."

Lottie only nodded, pushing the stroller beside Elisa's hands. "I really like to help, Auntie. I can help make one."

Elisa squinted in the distance. The sun finally stuck up for itself against the winter wonderland. Puddles pooled at low points of the concrete. She wanted to stay mad at that Sean Peters. But he really hadn't used Lottie. Lottie had all but invited him over to start building a playset. Sean had merely suggested they go to the park, and offered a discounted price on their own playset. But Elisa couldn't take on his need to work. She couldn't be responsible for one more person when her best effort to help her niece fell short compared to a stranger who'd taken the time to listen.

"Excuse me?" A cheery woman with bright

red cheeks and dyed blond curls spilling out from her woolen hat took careful steps down the sidewalk in front of Elisa's house. She was probably the age of Elisa's grandmother, but her vibrant blue eyes and smiling red lips painted her as energetic as a high school cheerleader.

"Um, hello." Elisa parked the stroller at the end of the driveway. "Are you Marge?" The basket in the woman's arms gave off a buttery aroma. Elisa remembered Sean's mention of her baking neighbor.

"I sure am." Her laugh bumbled out, and she dropped her gaze to Lottie. "And you must be the crafty sculptor who created such a beautiful snow family in the backyard."

Lottie tilted her head. "Are you a spy?"

Marge tossed her head back in a sweet chuckle. "Oh, no, I am just your neighbor, Miss Marge. You can't really see where my yard ends and yours begins. There's never been a fence between our houses in the forty years I've lived here."

"Is that so?" Elisa hadn't realized that. She'd had every intention of incorporating a fence when she'd dreamed of Chad's backyard oasis. Marge just raised her eyebrows as if waiting for a response. "Hello, I am Elisa Hartley. These are my nieces—Lottie and Ava."

Marge's eyes twinkled as she looked at the

girls. She lifted the napkin, but then hesitated and gave a questioning look to Elisa. "Do you mind if I offer a little treat? The whole basket is for you all, but a snack is always a nice end to a walk, don't you think?"

"Oh, sure, that's okay." Elisa turned the stroller so Ava could face Marge. She pulled out a snickerdoodle cookie for each girl. When Marge offered one to Elisa, she declined and turned the stroller back toward the house.

"Go on, dear. I'll follow you and carry in these goodies. Your hands are full."

This was awkward. The woman was practically inviting herself over. Elisa had lived in a loft filled with busy professionals for so long, she wasn't used to such social neighbors. She couldn't help but think life might be way different without the girls around. They certainly attracted do-gooders.

"Now, Elisa, tell me you've got Lottie signed up at St. George's Preschool? It is the best in town and just down the street."

"Actually, I do not. That was on my list of things to do—well, childcare is, anyway. I head to the office twice a week—about an hour away." She'd used up all her vacation and personal time back in December. These past two months she'd worked online by the grace of her very empathetic boss at Innovations Design. Mom and Elisa had agreed that since Ava didn't go to childcare when her parents were alive, she would stay home as much as possible—at least during the transition. So, the perfect childcare arrangement was a question lurking amid the many things Elisa needed to sort out.

"I highly recommend St. George's." Marge climbed the steps to the front door carefully, breathed out a heavy huff, then flashed a wide smile. "My daughter is the preschool director. And they have a toddler program for the little one."

"Ah, I see." Elisa fished her keys out of the stroller cup holder. "I will look into it, Marge. I had only considered day care."

"Oh, it's a great program. Those kiddos can write their names by Thanksgiving." She winked. "I have a great-granddaughter who is near genius." Her words were spoken like any doting grandmother should—with not one bit of sarcasm or humor. Completely serious about her kin's intellect.

"I know what my name looks like!" Lottie pushed the door open after Elisa turned the key. "Come in, Miss Marge. I will show you."

"Ah, not right now, Lottie." Elisa was not going to be forced into more conversation because of an overly social four-year-old. "Ava needs a nap. But maybe next time—"

"Yes, yes. Next time. Maybe when I throw you a welcome party," Marge declared.

Elisa rolled the stroller inside and then took the basket. "Oh, that won't be necessary."

"Why, it's a tradition!" Marge tipped her nose up. "Don't worry, you won't have to host. The Rapid Falls knitters like to meet at Sweet Lula's and buy coffee and pastries for newcomers." The lady shielded her mouth with her hand as if she were hiding her words from…the rest of the neighborhood. "I provide most of the shop's American pastries. Lula, my very best friend, only bakes Greek cookies. Delicious, but we've sweetened the menu with variety." Another syrupy chuckle erupted from Marge. "Pardon the pun."

"Sounds delightful. I have a lot to take care of right now. We'll talk soon." Elisa guided Lottie indoors as the little girl waved to Marge. Marge called out a goodbye in singsong, and Elisa closed the door at last.

Elisa had absolutely no desire to sit with a bunch of women eating sweets. She didn't even have time for that. But the preschool idea was something she would definitely look into.

"Maybe the preschool has a good playset, Lottie." She began to take off Ava's hat and gloves while Lottie peered at the goodies in Marge's basket. "We'll go check it out first thing tomorrow."

"Did Mr.—uh…that guy…build it, too?"

"I really don't know."

"I'll ask him next time we see him."

Lottie was pushing Elisa into future conversations already. The two little girls ran into the playroom, their little voices echoing slightly off the hardwood floors.

Elisa admired Lottie's and Ava's enthusiasm around others. She wasn't quite as extroverted as her half brother's children. Her stomach soured as she thought of her abrupt departure from Sean. He wasn't trying to weasel business from her—but he was honest that the project she'd promised meant something to him. There was no way she could follow through with it. She looked around the old four-season room that had toys scattered everywhere, nothing like the posh transition space to the backyard that she'd planned.

Elisa caught sight of her calendar counting down to her first day back at Innovations Design. Ugh, her boss had paid for her house to be added to the Northern Iowa Tour of Remodeled Homes this summer. How would she manage to finish up the projects here, settle in with two children, work and avoid adding to her Rapid Falls social calendar? A backyard upheaval just seemed like the last thing she should permit.

Elisa hardly felt in control. Marge didn't help—sweet as she was. Elisa really hadn't thought about making connections so quickly. But what else could she expect from such a quaint small town like Rapid Falls? And besides, these new acquaintances seemed to know what was best for her nieces—a playset and preschool.

What would be thrown at her next?

Chapter Four

Elisa called the preschool first thing the next morning and set up a tour. The director, Marge's daughter, emitted the same cheery tone as her mother, even over the cell phone. The girls were easy to bundle up and buckle in the car with the promise of seeing other children.

St. George's Preschool was housed in an annex of a turn-of-the-century church building with red bricks and a tall bell tower shadowing a play yard off the parking lot.

"Look! They have a swirly slide." Lottie bounced in her car seat while Elisa tried to unbuckle her.

"That's exciting, but I need you to sit still for a sec." Elisa managed to unhook the five-point harness with the squirmy child squealing in her ear.

"I want to go play!"

"Me, too!" Ava kicked her little heels against the seat.

"Let's see if the director will let you." Elisa helped Lottie down and kept a firm grip on her hand as they walked around to unbuckle Ava. "I wonder if it's even dry." Lumps of old snow lined the bottom of the chain-link fence. The door to the building swung open, and a teacher emerged leading a line of children, all about Lottie's size. The teacher took an old towel and wiped down the equipment while the children began to run around the play yard in snow boots.

Lottie wiggled her hand from Elisa's and ran to the fence across from the slide the teacher was drying. "'Scuse me! What's your name?" Her little gloved hands curled onto the wire of the fence.

The woman looked up and waved. "Hi, there! I am Miss Priya."

"Can I come in?"

Elisa quickly helped Ava down and spoke to the teacher over Lottie's hat bobble. "No worries. We have a meeting with Mrs. Barlow." She offered an apologetic smile and carefully withdrew Lottie's hand from the fence. "Lottie, have you ever met a stranger?"

"Oh, no, Auntie. I'm not allowed to talk to strangers." Her eyes were big and serious. Elisa chuckled, wondering what constituted as a stranger in the little girl's mind. They continued to the front door while Lottie waved to Miss Priya.

Jane Barlow met them at the front desk of the preschool. She was several years older than Elisa but had the same youthful disposition as Marge. She bent over, plastering her hands on her knees so she was near eye level with Lottie and Ava. "Hello, girls. I am Mrs. Jane. How are you liking Rapid Falls?"

"It's wet," Ava offered.

Jane laughed and straightened. She held out her hand for a firm shake from Elisa. "She's not wrong. I am Jane. Where did you all move from?"

"We spent January in Grangewood near Des Moines. But the girls are from Austin, Texas."

"Ah, yes, I can see how our soggy start to spring might make an impression on them." Jane crossed to some steps that spanned the entire width of the lobby. "Follow me."

Elisa admired the bright windows flanked by walls with backpacks and coats on hooks. "This is a sunny lobby. I love the original window casements."

"They're nice. But we're trying to come up with an accessible solution for the space," Jane explained as she led them up the steps. "It's been difficult since we have a student in a wheelchair trying to access different levels of a building that hasn't been touched since the doors opened in 1951." They entered a hallway with faded carpeting.

"I could see how that would be a necessity. Does the church fund your program?"

"Yes, and they are so generous. We're going to start a campaign for the building fund. But we haven't quite figured out how we would adjust to fit our needs."

"Have you spoken to an architect?" Elisa examined the area behind them.

Jane shook her head.

"I work in a design firm," Elisa explained. "They don't specialize in this type of project, but a designer would know what could fit your needs." She eyed the problematic stairs. "I am sure you could make something work. That wall over there is probably not load-bearing. Taking it down would give you tons of possibilities."

"Wow, thanks for the tip. It's hard to move forward sometimes." Jane flipped on a switch in a classroom. "I might need to invite you to the next board meeting."

"I love to problem-solve." Elisa shrugged her shoulders as her cheeks warmed. And while little Miss Lottie was just fine introducing herself to random people, Elisa was more comfortable getting to know the potential of a space—or a house—or what the future held for a place. What was it that Chad had often said? *"Lees, you have more inanimate friends than I have living and breathing ones."* A silly joke. And now, a tiny jab in her heart that maybe she'd missed the chance to focus on the people around her. She ran her hand on top of Ava's knit cap. At least she'd had a couple of good conversations with her half brother, Charlie, and his wife, Sylvia, during that week she'd visited last year. If only they'd been close their whole lives. Elisa pushed aside her unwelcome emotion and focused on guiding the girls as they followed Jane into a colorful classroom.

After Jane explained the daily routines, and Elisa managed to keep Ava and Lottie from an enticing art corner filled with bins of glue, paints and markers, they toured the parents'-day-out area of the school.

"The toddler program keeps the same schedule as the preschool, nine to three p.m., but it's open only on Tuesdays and Thursdays. Gives parents a chance to run errands or work while all their littles are cared for." Jane tapped Ava on the nose.

After they finished the tour, Jane wove them back down the steps to the front lobby. "The girls can start as soon as you'd like. We have space for both."

"Can we go to the playground now?" Lottie reached up to push on the door. Elisa gently grabbed her hand.

"Our three-year-old class is heading out there in a few minutes," Jane said. "But just down the street is the city park. The playground is fantastic."

Sean had mentioned that he had designed the playground area. Maybe the park was just what Lottie needed. "We'll check it out. Do you recommend any day cares? I am going to need to commute at least two days a week, so I'll need care after preschool dismissal."

"We have a list. Just a minute." Jane rummaged through the drawers of a desk that looked like it may have been built right alongside the old annex building. "We must have given away our last copy. I am pretty sure City Hall has a bunch printed."

Lottie was now tugging at Elisa's sleeve, and Ava had her nose pressed against the glass of the door. "Oh, Ava, don't do that." She pulled her away and gave Jane an apologetic look.

"No worries. Cleaning button-size smudges is one of our specialties around here." Her tinkling laugh was no doubt inherited from her mother. Elisa recalled Marge's sweet countenance as she offered her delectable desserts. She made another mental note to send her a thank-you.

They emerged into the brisk morning, and before the door closed, Elisa turned around again. "Thank you, Jane. I will get their paperwork done as soon as possible."

"Bye, Ava and Lottie." Jane waved, and the two little girls returned a goodbye in loud, high-pitched unison.

While they drove away, the girls chatted about all they saw at the school and how excited they were to play there. At least part of Elisa's childcare dilemma was solved. She couldn't even consider life as a commuter until she had the girls in good care.

Chad had been wrong about her inanimate friends monopolizing her focus. She glanced in the rearview mirror at the two rosy-cheeked little girls. They were worth all her attention. She prayed she would continue to find good solutions for this new life together.

Sean had a productive morning checking in on the retirement center's gardens and prepping beds for the spring blooms. His work truck was filled with plant material and mulch. The scent awakened his senses to the joy of being in this business—even if he wasn't crafting up dynamic design, at least he was outside breathing the fresh air and offering the simple pleasure of colorful flowers around their town. He saved his biggest client, the city office, for the afternoon since Blythe was meeting him after school to make copies and pin up her flyers in the various Main Street shops.

City Hall, on the corner of Main and First, was the flagship building for all the smaller, unique buildings along Main. Once the Rapid Falls founder's residence, City Hall was a nod to the last half of the nineteenth century—dormer windows from a mansard roof, red brick and decorative trim above each window.

Sean pulled open the door and crossed over the marble lobby to the receptionist, Frida Jamison. She sat behind a polished desk the same chocolate color as the ornate trim that ambled along the paneled wainscot and up the stately stairs behind her.

"Hi, there, Frida." Sean pulled off his gloves and stuck them in the back pocket of his jeans.

"I was wondering when I'd be seeing you." The little woman with tightly curled gray hair pushed her laptop away and folded her hands. "We're all ready for some flowers in those barrels out there. Especially since the twinkle lights are no longer decorating the evergreens."

"Twinkle lights do wonders in a season when landscapers can't do much." Sean winked. "And yes, I've got bright plans for planting. Dropping off invoices." He handed her an envelope. The

Tour of Remodeled Homes flyer sat on her desk. "Are you thinking about touring, Frida? I think most of them are closer to Marion and Waterloo." The only one here was Elisa's house. The one project that would outshine twinkle lights, any day. But his ambition had soured after his last encounter with Elisa.

Frida slid the poster off her desk and stood. "Nah, I was asked to hang it up on the city board." She crossed from her desk to the wide bulletin board that filled the back wall. "I'd love to see inside that house on Birch Street, though."

Sean clenched his teeth, but had to admit, "It's pretty sophisticated, from what I've seen."

"How's the backyard coming along? Your dad always complimented your work." Frida's sympathetic gleam warmed Sean.

He shoved his hands in his pockets and rocked back on his heels. "It's not coming along at all." He fisted his palms. How could a fellow designer—especially a talented one like Elisa—not see the need for his work?

"That's strange. Marge said you'd been over there a few times." She plucked a thumbtack from the board and began to position the poster.

He gave a dry laugh. "Marge sees all. I was there mainly to move snow. The owner isn't wanting to move forward with the project." And he wasn't counting down the moments to bump into that woman again. After Elisa and the girls returned to their walk yesterday, he'd told himself to back off. She'd acted like he was a conniving salesperson. Maybe he shouldn't have mentioned the wholesale inventory. The last woman who'd treated him like he'd come on too strong had not only broken his heart—but crushed Blythe's, sending his sister into a dark season. His ex-girlfriend Kylie had gotten too close to his family only to pull away and blame Sean for smothering her. He'd thought Kylie was proof that he could form a trusting relationship after living for years under the cloud of his mother's abandonment. But in the end, Kylie had shown him that his strongest bonds were with his family rather than with a romantic partner.

Sure, Elisa was purely a potential business acquaintance—no heartstrings there—but Sean didn't like feeling so small in his own driveway—the same feeling when Kylie had pulled away from the house after they had broken up.

The door chimed behind him, and Blythe barreled into the lobby, her cheeks flushed and her smile wide. "Sean, you'll never guess what just happened. I already got a babysitting job!"

"Wow, that was fast."

"Saturday night. Maddy and Ty Jacobs."

Before the door closed, it was caught by the

boot of none other than Elisa Hartley. She turned to maneuver her stroller through the doorway.

"Oh, sorry," Blythe exclaimed, and held the door open the rest of the way.

Every muscle tensed in Sean's neck and jaw. He tried to soften and appear at least cordial without any sign of his earlier frustration. These Hartley ladies—tall and small—were new residents after all.

Lottie stopped beside Blythe and looked straight at Sean. She threaded her fingers together and with a sparkle in her big brown eyes said, "I like your playground."

"The one at the park?" He tossed a questioning look at Elisa.

She gave him a quick grin and handed Ava a sippy cup. "Yes. We went there before lunch. The girls thought it was great." Sean hooked an eyebrow—feeling a little more like the landscape architect needing approval from their design professor. She was not his boss. But he had been impressed with her work and wondered what she might think of his. It didn't matter what she thought now.

Elisa offered in a matter-of-fact tone, "You incorporated the terraced seating well."

"Thanks. It was a fun project," he managed to reply with the same matter-of-factness. Her hair was straight and long, and she wore just enough makeup to accentuate her doe eyes and add a rosy blush to her defined cheekbones. Not nearly as much as she had the day of her wedding. He shoved away the memory of her streaked face staring out the car window. A wave of compassion tripped up Sean's usual cool-as-an-Iowa-spring demeanor, and he found himself staring longer than he should.

Breaking the awkward silence, Sean turned his attention to Lottie. "What was your favorite part?"

"The swirly thingy." She drew a circle in the air, but Sean just shrugged his shoulders. "You know, the go-round thing?"

"Ah, the merry-go-round." He laughed.

"Yes." She pulled her hat off. Her dark hair clung to her face with static. She swept it away and leaned toward him. "Can you build one for me, Mr. Sean?" Lottie whispered.

Sean gave a shrug then reset his gaze at Elisa. She didn't seem to react to Lottie's words. *Good.* Sean could continue to inch away from yesterday's encounter. Elisa glanced his way. He said, "I assume you haven't been here yet. City Hall is nearly as exciting as the park—for an interior designer like yourself, Elisa."

"It's pretty nice in here. But I am more in guardian-mode these days." Elisa turned the stroller slightly as she perused the giant bulletin board spanning the back wall. "Definitely a cool building, though." She walked up to Frida. "Excuse me?"

Frida smoothed down the newly hung poster and grinned wide. "Elisa? Ah, you're Marge's new neighbor. What a coincidence, I was just hanging this up." Before Elisa could speak, Frida continued, "I hear your house is on the tour. How lovely." She grabbed Elisa's hand for a shake without hesitation. "I am Frida Jamison."

"Nice to meet you." Elisa's smile wasn't quite as wide as Frida's. Sean refrained from chuckling. There was a reason Frida worked at City Hall. She made introductions effortless on the part of any newcomer because she pretty much carried the conversation.

"Sean says you've made the house spectacular." Frida crossed over to Sean. "Or, what did you say, *sophisticated*?"

"Can't help but share a good thing when I see it," he said sheepishly.

Elisa's lips parted as if she would speak, but Frida continued, "And Sean's the guy for getting your grounds ready for the tour." Her little hand gave Sean's arm a squeeze.

Sean couldn't help but laugh. "Thanks for your confidence, Frida." *But not for your lack of discretion.* He patted her hand. Elisa's uneasy look was not lost on him. "I don't think our newest resident is looking for a landscape architect." He stepped away from the women and signaled to Blythe to follow him out the door. "See you all later."

Elisa cleared her throat and said to Frida, "The director of St. George's Preschool told me there was a childcare provider list here."

"At the far corner of the bulletin board. I think only a few have spaces at this point in the year."

Blythe froze and spun away from Sean. She skipped over to Elisa and waved at Lottie. "Hi, there. I just hung up my flyer here. I am Rapid Falls's best babysitter."

Sean cupped his hand over his mouth to refrain from laughing. As scared as Blythe could be about some things, his sister didn't have a shy bone in her body when it came to making new friends.

Elisa glanced over at Sean and grinned. "Related? I see the resemblance." They didn't have the same hair or eye color, so he assumed she referred to their persistence in offering their services. "I need more than a sitter, unfortunately." Elisa began to browse the sheet she unpinned from the board. "I am commuting to Marion."

Blythe continued, "Well, I am free every afternoon and on weekends."

Elisa took the flyer and studied it. "Every afternoon?"

"Sure," Blythe confirmed. "You're in the re-modeled Victorian, right? That's on my way home from school. Afternoons would be easy."

Elisa blew a stray hair from her nose. "Do you know how helpful that would be?" She offered a genuine smile to Blythe. Sean smiled, too—at his sister. At least one Peters was getting business. "I'll give you a call after I figure out my schedule, and you can let me know your rate."

Blythe opened her mouth to speak, then closed it. She turned to Sean and then back to Elisa again. "You know, I'd babysit for free if you'll hire my bro…"

Sean shook his head adamantly and squeezed Blythe's shoulder with a gentle don't-even-say-it warning. He recalled their conversation about bargaining for the landscape project. That was a joke. "Blythe will wait for your call."

Elisa hooked an eyebrow. "Okay. We'll chat soon."

Sean made a mental note to tell Blythe not to get her hopes up. Even though they'd lived here all their lives, after the awkward commercial pitch from Frida and Blythe's determination, Sean had a sinking feeling that when it came to Elisa Hartley, the Peterses had overstayed their welcome.

Chapter Five

The next afternoon, Elisa took a call from her boss while the girls were playing. "Hi, Gerard."

"Wanted to check in on the remodel. We had a client interested in incorporating a similar transitional space like what you are working on. Would love to send some pics to her. How is it coming along?"

"Oh. I was going to keep it as a traditional four-season room instead. We aren't going to do anything to the backyard right now."

"That's disappointing. Did the landscape architect fall through?"

No, not at all. Sean seemed to have roped his sister into scheming a way to get his crew on Elisa's property. "No, he's actually pretty eager. I just—I have so much going on with the girls I didn't want an added project to worry about."

"I understand you've been through a lot. But,

Elisa, this isn't really an added project—it's what we agreed to. Innovations doesn't allow the brand to be associated with any employee's home makeover. We've agreed to the tour because we trust your design. We expect the project you promised."

Elisa didn't like the word *promised.* She'd been burned by leaning too heavily into a promise. But Gerard was talking business, not wedding vows, and Elisa knew how much the firm counted on top-notch representation. And besides, she'd agreed to showcasing the house when it wasn't hers, and when she was a happy bride-to-be.

"You know, I've been in contact with the landscape architect. I'll see what we can come up with."

"That's good. And you're back in the office starting Tuesday?"

"Yes, Tuesdays and Thursdays. At home the rest of the week. Does that still work?" She held her breath. Those were the days that she had full childcare coverage.

"It will work for now." Gerard then whispered to someone. She'd had his attention for about five minutes. The typical length for a conversation with the ever-busy founder of Innovations Design.

"Great. See you, then."

Elisa ended the call. She couldn't help but feel the weight of all her responsibilities pressing down on her shoulders. And as much as she craved staying true to her introverted self while taking on the gargantuan task of mothering, she now had to figure out life with a construction crew and the very nonintroverted Peters siblings.

As Elisa headed over to the four-season room to check on the girls, the doorbell rang. She pivoted and stepped over some toddler-size Mary Janes and opened the door.

Blythe held hands with Lottie on the front porch.

"What are you doing out there?" Elisa immediately took Lottie's other hand. A couple of cars passed by, and a delivery truck turned at the corner. What if she'd gone in the street? "You know you are not allowed to be outside alone." They hurried into the foyer.

Blythe explained, "I figured she wasn't supposed to be out there when she waved at me on my way home from school." She then crouched down and swept her long strawberry blond hair over her shoulder. With a sobering look at Lottie, she affirmed, "That was smart to stay on the porch, though." Blythe tilted her head up and gleamed at Elisa. "I told her to wait for me, and she didn't move an inch toward the steps." Blythe popped up and tucked her hands under her backpack straps. "No harm done."

Elisa didn't feel so at ease. A million horrible

scenarios formed in her mind. "I appreciate you looking out for her, Blythe."

Blythe tapped Lottie on the nose. "You're welcome."

Elisa admired her confidence. "How old *are* you?" She seemed to be barely a teenager but sounded like a confident young adult.

Blythe giggled. "I'm thirteen."

"Wow, that's old!" Lottie exclaimed. "But not as old as Auntie." She cupped her hands over her mouth and chuckled.

Elisa narrowed her gaze at her niece, half in jest and half wondering how she was going to make sure Lottie stayed inside—especially with all sorts of construction mess coming up ahead. "Lottie Hartley, we have some serious talking to do, and it *is* because I am older. And wiser." Elisa ran her hand along Lottie's dark hair, thankful she was safe, then turned her attention to Blythe again. "Thank you for being wise also."

"You're welcome again." Blythe breezed through the door and turned around on the porch. "Have you found a sitter yet?" She rocked back on her heels, just like Sean had in City Hall. Elisa could see the resemblance. Both Blythe and Sean had friendly built into their DNA, it seemed.

"Actually, I have not. But I will need someone to pick up the girls from St. George's on Tuesdays and Thursdays. I suspect thirteen-year-olds don't have their driving licenses yet?"

Blythe shook her head. "But my brother might help out." She folded her arms across her chest and tilted her head with the most mischievous smirk. "You know…" She bit her lip, then pulled her shoulder back in a stance of confidence mixed with pride. "It would be really easy to convince him to help out if he was coming here, anyway—you know, to work on your backyard." She raised an eyebrow at Lottie, then muttered to Elisa, "The first thing you might need is a playset to keep her contained."

Elisa laughed. "Oh, really? Are you sure you're in the babysitting business and not in marketing?"

Blythe offered an enthusiastic grin. "Sean's been hoping for this project to help our family business. You should see how excited he gets when he discusses his ideas. And my college fund." She rolled her eyes.

Elisa steeled her gaze on the girl. She knew Blythe was genuine. And if she hadn't just ended the call with Gerard, Elisa would probably have cut this conversation short at the first mention of Sean's business. But everything had changed. Elisa's control of the environment and their privacy was inevitably weakening by every breath of the Rapid Falls spring air.

"Can you give me Sean's number?" Elisa pulled her phone from her pocket. "Maybe we can work something out." Elisa winked. "Hopefully, you get commission for your sales pitches, Blythe."

Blythe shrugged her shoulders. "A babysitting job is commission, enough." She winked back.

Wow, sales talent starts at a young age with the Peterses, it seems. But truly, Elisa was impressed with the tenacity and maturity of the young girl, and fervently thankful that Blythe had walked by their house just in time to stop a potential disaster from happening.

Sean turned onto Birch Street on his way to Waterloo to return the flagstone he'd purchased for Elisa's house. He'd lose some money on the materials, but at least it wasn't taking up space in the warehouse next to Dad's old Mustang, reminding him that he had to drop the account before even breaking ground. Sean decided it was time to start branching out beyond Rapid Falls. Not ideal with Blythe's unease about being home alone at night. Maybe Sean should wait to expand until the summer's longer daylight hours? But their business ledger was quickly fading from black to a dismal red. He needed to figure out something fast.

He tried to drive by Elisa's without his usual

designer eye studying the space between Marge's vegetable garden and Elisa's property line. The Griffins had mentioned installing a fence to link up with the existing one on the other side of the house. But knowing Marge's pride in the history of the two properties being undivided, Sean had figured that finding a good solution between the two yards was a priority in his concept.

Not his concept anymore.

His attention was drawn away from the bare garden plot to Elisa's front porch. Was that Blythe? He slowed the truck along the curb and rolled down his window.

Elisa was at the door, and Blythe turned to go. When she saw Sean's truck, she jumped around again. "He's here," Sean heard her say.

The tall blonde woman widened the door and joined Blythe on the porch in fuzzy socks. She lifted her arm in a quick wave, while Blythe motioned for him to join them. "Come here, Sean!"

His sister had no doubt landed another babysitting account. Sean chuckled as he parked and made his way up the driveway. Blythe was something else. Bright and full of life. An answer to prayer after her bout of panic attacks when Kylie left.

"Hello, ladies," Sean greeted.

"Hey, there," Elisa replied.

Blythe bounced on her toes. "I'm gonna start

sitting for Elisa in the afternoons." Her eyes flashed with her usual enthusiasm. "And…"

Elisa stepped forward. "And, Sean, I am going to need to hire you after all."

Sean's heart throbbed in his throat. Did he hear her correctly? He shifted his gaze between his sister and Elisa.

Blythe grabbed at his arm and beamed at him. "Only if you can pick up the girls from preschool on Tuesdays and Thursdays, right, Elisa?"

Elisa laughed. "Your sister is quite a bargainer." Sean gaped at Blythe. He was used to people not holding up their end of the bargain— his ex, his mom, uh, even Elisa Hartley. He'd felt the weight of holding fast to his end of the deal for his sister—keeping her safe, healthy and thriving. Especially since he'd caused her breakdowns a couple years ago. But Blythe was helping *him* now? His sister amazed him more and more.

"Whatever it takes for the family biz, right, Sean?" She bobbed her eyebrows just like Dad would. Sean's throat tightened, and he pushed away the usual waves of remorse for Dad missing out and the resentment of Mom choosing to stay away.

Elisa continued, "The biggest stipulation is that we need it finished before May first." Lottie and Ava appeared at the door. Elisa lifted Ava to her hip. "And also, your crew can't disturb nap time." She kissed Ava's temple. "So, what do you say? Can you squeeze our backyard into your schedule?"

Lottie held her hands against her chest in supplication. "You build a playset for us, Mr. Sean?"

"I guess that would be another stipulation," Elisa chimed in. "Make it kid-friendly for our practical use. Think you can manage sophisticated toddler entertainment?"

Sean rubbed his hands together. "Absolutely." He smiled at Lottie. "I think I can figure out a playset and a perfect patio, too."

"Yippee!" Lottie yanked on Ava's little feet, and the two-year-old squirmed out of Elisa's arms and toddled behind her sister into the house again. Lottie's high-pitched voice rattled on about a swirly slide.

Elisa watched the girls disappear, then turned to Sean. "There are so many balls in the air right now. Preschool, day care, work—" She glanced at Blythe. "And now the stakes are raised on this remodel. I wasn't even planning on moving here, but then I got the girls in January—" A tweak of uncertainty pulled the corners of her mouth down.

"Didn't you buy the house back in the fall?" Blythe inquired.

A rosy shade filled Elisa's cheeks. "Oh, yes.

Um, plans changed several times between then and now."

Sean wasn't looking at his new employer now—but at the downcast bride and the grieving sister.

Elisa's explanation carried the effects of all those changed plans—a slight quiver in her voice and a hurried get-it-out-and-over-with rambling. Sean knew that response well. Blythe would often try to dig deeper to sort out the reasons that people they loved didn't love them enough to stay—Mom and Kylie, to be specific. Sean had just wanted to leave behind their past circumstances and gain some stability in their present situation. After enough of his generalized responses and changing the subject, Blythe had stopped asking. Good thing, because life was becoming more complicated now that Mom was sick and needing money. He couldn't tell Blythe and risk her falling apart again.

Blythe seemed fine now. She never mentioned Kylie, and hardly talked about Mom. He was thankful. Relieved. And he would give Elisa some reprieve from her own circumstance by focusing only on his role in her life now—not as a guest of the groom, but as her dedicated landscape architect and, it seemed, her nieces' chauffeur?

A very happy bargain, indeed.

Chapter Six

Thursday was a big day for the Hartley girls. Preschool for the littles, and the knitting club's welcome for reluctant Elisa. Marge had invited Elisa while she was outside inspecting the old patio and brainstorming a seamless transition between the patio and the four-season room. The woman wouldn't take no for an answer, so Elisa finished up some work and forced herself to be social.

She called her mom and talked on the way to Sweet Lula's. "The girls seemed fine at drop-off, Mom." Elisa parked her car in a space near the corner coffee shop. "They ran right into their classrooms."

"Good. This will bring them some routine. It's good to be around their peers." Mom's approval came through the car speaker, and Elisa wished she was heading to meet *her* for coffee instead of a roundtable of strangers. "And you are off to a knitting club?"

"The knitters are hosting a welcome for me. Totally my kind of thing, right?"

"Believe it or not, Lees, it's good for you to be around people, too."

Elisa's sarcasm had clearly met Mom on the other end of the phone call.

"Oh, don't worry. Lottie and Ava have kept me social." Elisa couldn't believe that she knew so many people on a first-name basis here in Rapid Falls. Back in Marion, she hadn't known anyone outside her office, and she'd lived there for four years. Elisa liked keeping to herself. She was perfectly content with some books, a few unfinished drawings to work on and a good long while with her own thoughts. That was why it had been easy with Chad. He was the same way—self-sufficient in quiet company. At least, Elisa had assumed he was perfectly content in their downtime together. What kind of introvert went off on a Caribbean business trip and was swept away by a tanned beauty? Heat crept up her neck. Maybe she hadn't given Chad a reason to stay. Boring nights-in in a potential family home or parasailing over blue waters with an exotic princess? The choice must've been clear to Chad. Elisa shook her head.

"Elisa? Are you there?"

"Oh, yeah, sorry, Mom. I better go."

"Okay, sweetie. Call me after the girls get home."

"Sure will."

Elisa turned off her car, plopped her phone in her purse and stepped into the bright morning sunshine. Rapid Falls Main Street had a storybook feel—old-fashioned streetlamps, newly planted flowers in round barrels dotting the sidewalks, and eclectic storefronts with canopies over doorways and shutters in different colors.

Through the big picture window, the coffee shop inside appeared busy with customers. How many were waiting on her? Her palms grew sweaty as she considered the last time a room full of people had waited on her. And the complete humiliation and heartbreak that followed. Although only her getaway driver had witnessed her full-blown breakdown. He was kind enough to let her grieve without speaking most of the way to her parents' house.

She took a deep breath and pushed the glass door. The rich coffee aroma immediately awakened Elisa to the charm of the place, pushing aside her anxiety. Black-and-white checkered flooring, dainty round tables accented with painted flowerpots with handmade flowers in various fabric patterns.

"Elisa! Over here!" Marge waved from the

back corner. Her neighbor stood with a gaggle of women between a glass case of baked items and a few tables pushed up together.

Elisa wove through and spotted Frida from City Hall. The other six women were unfamiliar, but bright-eyed and smiling. *You can do this, Lees. You aren't the awkward bride. You are the mysterious newbie.*

Marge immediately rushed up to her and threaded her hand around Elisa's elbow. "Now, you order whatever you'd like. It's on us. Oh, and Lula's made up a special platter just for you. Here she is."

A four-foot-something woman came around the glass case with a dainty dish piled high with various cookies and pastries. She was several inches shorter than Marge. The two women had the same hairdo, short and perfectly coiffed, but Lula's was a dyed chestnut color instead of Marge's golden platinum.

"You must be Elisa. So nice to meet you." Lula's Greek accent was warm and rolling. Her brown eyes sparkled with genuine hospitality. "Come, come, sit." She nodded to a seat and the women on either side scooted apart.

As soon as Elisa sat down, the group gathered up their knitting and placed it in baskets under their seats. They began to introduce themselves and insisted she try one of each of the treats in front of her. Not much resistance from Elisa. The powdered sugar dusting the sweet treats enticed her to take a bite. The buttery cookie melted in her mouth and gave her something to do with her hands—an often-unresolved matter when she met new people.

After Elisa ordered some tea, she answered questions about her job as an interior designer and elaborated on her house's updates. The spritely Susie Fredrickson, sporting an athletic pullover and a messy bun of salt-and-pepper hair, began to explain her daughter's new property. "Could I get your business card, Elisa? Her house is going to be fabulous, but she's at a loss on how to pull the rooms together. What was it she said…uh…something about elegant but cozy."

"Oh, I am pretty sure our firm is booked right now." Elisa picked at the doily on the platter.

"Well, how about you?" Susie asked. "She probably doesn't need a whole firm. Just someone with exceptional taste." She winked. "She'll pay, of course."

Elisa gave a curt smile and ignored her tightening chest at the prospect of one more thing on *her* platter. "Let me get settled in. You know where to find me." She giggled and set off a domino of polite laughter around the table. Did she just invite the town to knock on her door for design advice? She cleared her throat, trying to think of something to say that didn't have to do with her.

Lula came over with a pretty teacup and teapot. "Here you go. Earl Grey." Elisa loved the way she rolled her *r*'s.

"Thank you."

Lula patted her shoulder and disappeared behind the glass case again.

Before Elisa could change the subject, Tina Delaney, a tall, confident woman with a pixie cut and pointy readers, took the honors. "So, I assume you've met the debonair Sean Peters, then?"

The ladies shifted in their seats and leaned in. All eyes on Elisa.

"The landscape architect? Actually, he's going to work on our backyard." She poured the tea in her cup.

"Very good." Tina drummed her fingers beside her own coffee mug. "He deserves every ounce of success. Professional and, well…"

"Personal?" Marge blurted, and her dimple grew deep with a dazzling smile as a titter of laughter went around the table. "Yes, yes, he does deserve his success. Especially after Kylie. And Howard and—" Marge hesitated and passed knowing glances around the table. "Well, all they've been through. But if anyone could make the most out of life, it's Howard's kids."

The entire group nodded in agreement.

Marge continued to explain to Elisa, "Howard, Sean and Blythe's father, was a wonderful man. Always helping his neighbors and this town. When he entered a room, he'd just steal the show because of his gregarious voice and amazing attitude."

"Speaking of entering a room," Tina interrupted, and rose to her feet. "Hello, Sean! Come join us." Her voice rose an octave or two. She appeared nearly smitten with the guy who made their way toward them.

Elisa couldn't blame Tina for her change from interviewer to admirer. Sean had a way of walking in his father's shoes, if what Marge said was accurate, with his genuine smile and confident stride. He greeted the women, who, in turn, sat up a little straighter and beamed a little brighter.

"We were just talking about you," Tina exclaimed. "Telling our newest resident that she'll not regret hiring you."

"Oh, really?" He pushed his glasses up on his nose and cast a hazel gaze toward Elisa. "Was she concerned?" He raised a brow, and a smile tugged at his mouth's corner.

"Not at all," Elisa said, and flicked her hair

over her shoulder. "You come highly recommended."

"He is quite the catch, isn't he, ladies?" Marge patted his arm while Elisa tried to not choke on the next bite of cookie. Marge noticed Elisa's wide-eyed look and corrected herself. "A catch for anyone looking for a landscape architect." She dipped her chin in satisfaction. Lula took Sean's order while all the knitters chatted among themselves. Elisa sipped her tea, planning her exit now that the attention had shifted from her to Sean. Although, she felt she was dangerously close to sharing the spotlight with Sean in a way that would cast them less as colleagues and more as a prospective…

Oh, she could not even consider that.

The knitters' club had an air of matchmaking about them, and if Elisa was wise, she'd hop out of this chair and leave. She glanced up at Sean, who continued to talk with Lula and now Marge. Debonair was right, but not a tempting trait for a woman who'd recently suffered an upended happily-ever-after. Allowing herself to depend on another person had left Elisa humiliated in the end. She had learned her lesson, and the only people who deserved her attention were her nieces. Being an adequate guardian may take her time and energy, too, but Lottie and Ava were worth it. Her love life was happily dormant.

"Elisa was just sharing that you are working on her yard. I am so excited to see you every day," Marge cooed. "Aren't you, Elisa?" Her blue eyes shaded with mischief.

"Oh, well…" *No, actually, I hadn't even considered it.*

Sean cleared his throat and said in a deeper voice than usual, "Speaking of the yard, I have some catalogs in the truck that I wanted to run past you, Elisa. Want to step outside while Miss Lula gets my order ready?"

"Yes!" Elisa's enthusiasm was no doubt noted by the women as something more than glee at the chance to escape. But she didn't look around, simply scooted her chair out and popped up next to Sean. He was only a couple inches taller than her.

Sean leaned over the glass case and called into the back, "I'll be right back, Miss Lula." He led the way through the coffee shop and out the front door, the tinkling bell mixing with the quiet chatter of the matchmaking club disguised as a welcome committee.

Sean flung open the passenger door of his pickup, which was parked along the sidewalk in front of Sweet Lula's. He reached in and pulled out a binder, then turned around and leaned against the passenger seat. Elisa hooked a hand on the open car door.

Sean flipped the pages. "There are several options for a playset that won't stick out like a sore thumb amid the more sophisticated design elements." He turned the binder around so Elisa could look at the rustic wood playsets.

"That's great." She sighed loudly, barely skimming the catalog page, and glanced at her watch. "I trust whatever you think is best. I am just glad to get some fresh air. I'm not one for crowds—especially such tight-knit ones." Amusement gleamed in her eyes. "Pardon the pun."

He shut the binder. "Don't let those women get to you. It's kinda their job to make sure the new girl is aware of all the eligible bachelors here. But they are mistaken. I am not one of them. My nights are booked with helping Blythe with her homework and a good read."

Elisa stared at him for a moment, then waved a dismissive hand. "As much as I am the new girl, that is the farthest thing from my mind, too. I just want to focus on the girls." She smiled, her eyes gleaming. "And a good read. Cozy mysteries are the best."

Sean laughed, dropping his gaze to the binder. "Nonfiction for me. Getting lost in someone else's facts and figures helps me relax after a weekend of being a caregiver. Besides that, there's not a lot of time to worry about…more trivial matters."

Elisa hooked an eyebrow, but the corners of her mouth tugged down slightly.

Trivial? Maybe not the best word for matters of the heart, especially to a woman whose groom had left her a few months ago. After his breakup with Kylie, Sean understood how lengthy the healing process could be. The rejection had changed him for good. He had become a little more cynical, a little more dependent on work to fulfill him—or at least distract him from what everyone thought was the natural progression in this life: boy meets girl, they fall in love, and they live happily ever after. A fairy tale for sure. One that the knitting club seemed committed to as their first order of business with Elisa. He wondered if she'd told the ladies about her almost wedding?

With another sigh, Elisa said, "The knitters also mentioned how much respect they have for your family. Your dad sounds like he was an amazing person." She folded her arms across her sweater. "We have that in common. Great dads."

Sean smiled. "Dad's death left a huge absence in Rapid Falls. He was the best. Especially with Blythe. Now I am all she has. It's tough raising a kid when it wasn't long ago that I felt like a kid myself."

"I've never felt so much like an adult, but now I have Lottie questioning me every day,

You take good care of us, Auntie?" She giggled, then tucked her hair behind her ear. Her brown eyes leveled with his gaze, and she continued, "It's good you had an example from your dad. I have about a month's worth of observing my father and mother as grandparents and a week's visit to my brother's last year under my belt. But the last person my parents raised was me."

"So, your brother was older than you?"

She nodded, then squinted into the bright day, opening her mouth as if to speak but thinking better of it.

"Honestly, Dad did such a good job with Blythe that I think it's easier for me." Sean tossed the binder back in the truck. "And that's just like my father—leaving a lasting impression that outshines any alternative. Makes it easier to follow his footsteps. But, man, I miss him." He pushed off the seat and shoved his hands in his pockets while Elisa stepped back. "How are the girls doing…with all that's happened?"

"They seem okay. There are moments—" Elisa bit her lip, then grimaced. "Moments when they just seem overwhelmed by something, and I can't figure out how to help them. Like, I had put juice in a sippy cup. Ava kept pushing it off the table and refusing to drink. It wasn't until Lottie walked in and informed me—as she is so good at doing—" Elisa's smirk was adorable evidence of the amusement Lottie-the-spitfire seemed to stir up. "That juice goes with a straw, not a sipper. How was I supposed to know that? Her parents had established the way—and I have to stumble across the dos and don'ts, as *trivial* as they are." Ah, she used the word in a much better context than he had.

"So, I take it you weren't around to observe them with their parents much?"

"Nope. Charlie and Sylvia moved to Texas when I was still in high school. I visited them for the first time last year."

"It sounds like the girls had great parents. I mean, a dad who builds a playset? Your brother followed in your dad's footsteps, I assume?" He returned a sideways smile as he closed the door. They began to walk back to the café. Elisa didn't say anything. Maybe she was preparing herself to reenter the matchmaker forum. Sean, for one, didn't feel threatened in the least. He'd told himself long ago that a relationship just wasn't worth the risk of throwing him off course for Blythe, the business and his pretty unrepairable heart.

Chapter Seven

Elisa wasn't expecting the wave of remorse that followed her from Sean's truck to the coffee shop. Charlie was gone and had left a gap in her family, maybe as sizable as Sean's father seemed to have left in this community. However, all sorts of unresolved matters remained after Charlie's death—especially for her father. Charlie had been resentful from a young age, after his mom had filed for divorce when he was eight years old. Three years before Elisa was born. While Elisa was growing up, her tenderhearted father had often striven to repair his relationship with his son, but every rejection by Charlie had only set Dad's gloominess for the following days. Elisa had learned early on that emotions destroyed peace. As a child, she'd retreat to books and drawing when the air grew thick with Dad's sorrow. And as she grew, con-

trolling her own emotions had become a tro-
phy in her heart. Chad had destroyed her in that
way—rejecting her to the point of obliterating
the composure she'd coveted and worked toward
for years.

At least Sean assured her that the matchmaking endeavor was not personal—just knitting
club habit. On a big gulp of air, Elisa wove her
way back to the table. The women had retrieved
their knitting again. A few looked at her over
their spectacles as she approached. Lula appeared with Sean's order—two to-go cups and
a large cake box.

Elisa didn't sit but curled her fingers on her
chairback. "Thank you so much for the welcome today. I have to pick up the girls from St.
George's soon."

Marge exclaimed, "Jane told me about your in-
sights for their annex building. You are just drum-
ming up business all over town. What with Susie's
daughter's house, too." She smiled at Susie.

The cheerful countenance Elisa had crafted
became strained. "Oh, no, no business. My firm
has a whole different scope—"

Sean stood beside her again. "Business?
What's this?"

Marge leaned over her purple-and-fuchsia
yarn. "The St. George's board could use a designer's eye. That's all."

Sean bobbed his head and steadied the box in his hand. "That's a good idea."

Maybe being on the board of St. George's Preschool would be another way for Elisa to help the girls. She didn't know much about preschoolers, so exposure to the behind-the-scenes work might be helpful. But that constriction in her chest told her that she was already wearing herself thin.

"Maybe one day. But right now, I need to get in a good rhythm with work and the girls." She offered Marge and the other women a wide smile, then turned to Sean as he balanced his to-go order. "I'll help you with the door." Elisa thanked the group again and followed Sean back through the shop.

Once they were outside, Elisa headed the opposite direction of his truck. Her car was parked a few spots down.

"You've made a great impression on those ladies," Sean called out.

"They are very—very welcoming." Elisa bounced her eyebrows and laughed. Somehow, she'd made a reputation for herself as a sought-after designer after one brief conversation with a preschool director. "I seem to recall you saying something about how this town wasn't so small that my business would be everyone's?"

He clamped his mouth shut and gave an apologetic shrug. "Just you wait until the girls start in the elementary school. They'll be in and out of everyone's backyards playing tag and hide-and-seek. And you will be completely indoctrinated as a Rapid Falls resident."

"Wow, I haven't thought that far ahead. We are just trying to make it to summer. But I am glad for the welcome, truly. This is the girls' new beginning." She took a couple of steps backward. "And mine." Elisa gave a quick wave to Sean, swiveled around and headed to her car.

Mom was right; it was good to be around people. And she was especially thankful they didn't try to dig into her personal life—although they nudged her toward a new one. At least Sean called out the matchmaking as typical and nothing to take seriously. That made it seem less threatening and more of a quirk among the knitting club. Elisa could handle quirks. She just didn't want to have to explain her disastrous love life to anyone. New beginnings meant a chance to know people without always deciphering the pity from the kindness.

On Tuesday morning, Elisa's stomach rolled with nerves as she got ready to commute to Marion. This would also be the first full day apart from the girls in two months. She eyed them through her bathroom mirror. Ava and Lottie sat in the middle of Elisa's bed watching cartoons.

Last night had been exceptionally sleepless because Lottie'd had nightmares. Eventually, the girls had fallen asleep in her bed around four in the morning. But Elisa had stayed awake, praying for protection over the girls while she was an hour's drive away today.

As she finished applying her makeup, her cell phone dinged. At first, she thought it was the TV in her room. But from the corner of her eye, she saw the screen light up and picked up her phone.

Sean had texted, We're still on for me to drop off supplies this morning?

Elisa replied, Yes. We'll be out of here by 8. The driveway is all yours. And you are okay with grabbing the girls from school at 3:30?

Sure thing.

"Can we go to work with you?" Lottie crawled across the quilt. "I don't want Mr. Sean to pick us up after school."

Elisa set down her phone. "Why not? I thought you liked him. He's building your playset, you know."

Lottie slid down the bed and walked into the bathroom where Elisa stood at the sink. "His truck is scary," she whispered, her bottom lip quivering.

Elisa crouched down so she was face-to-face

with Lottie. "It's actually really safe, I promise." Was Lottie thinking about her parents' accident? Charlie had been driving a truck. "Do you think it would help if I rode with you in the truck this first time?"

Her eyes lit up, and she nodded ferociously. "Yes! Yes, please." She clutched her arms around Elisa's neck. "I want you to go with us, Auntie," she whispered, her breath tickling Elisa's skin. Elisa squeezed back. She'd never been much of a hugger. But Ava and Lottie had changed her indifference toward the gesture. Each embrace they offered without her asking gave her more and more assurance that—no matter the house or the town they lived in—Elisa was meant to be part of their lives or, more definitely, the girls were meant to be part of hers.

For the first time in her career, something challenged her desire to work. And even more than that, she surprised herself by not feeling one bit of hesitation to reach out to the resident landscape architect and ask another favor. Usually, she'd problem-solve ways to not depend on one other person, and she certainly wouldn't ask a colleague to help with a personal errand. But she couldn't sense any shrinking back from the idea forming in her mind. What had happened to the reserved and self-sufficient Elisa Hartley? She could only blame it on this unexpected love for her brother's kids. She gulped back emotion and picked up her cell phone. "I'll call Mr. Sean and see if he can take us to preschool this morning. How about it?" Lottie jumped up and down and nearly knocked Elisa back into the wall. "Whoa!"

"Sorry, Auntie."

"It's okay, sweetie." Elisa laughed and straightened her blouse as she stood. A voice came through the phone. She'd accidentally called Sean already. She put the phone to her ear. "Hello?"

"I didn't realize we were at the point of using terms of endearment. *Sweetie* isn't my top choice, though." Sean's voice was thick with amusement.

"Ha ha." Elisa rolled her eyes but blushed at the sentiment. "I didn't mean to press Call so soon, but I did mean to call."

"I am looking forward to getting started today. Have any questions?"

"Actually, I have a favor to ask you—if you have time on your hands this morning."

"Your house is the only thing on my list."

While Lottie ran over to the step stool positioned for her to climb onto the bed, Elisa explained the situation to Sean. He was happy to drive them. They ended the call, and Elisa quickly finished her makeup, feeling oddly at ease by Sean's willingness to help. Single parenting was not a simple task, and having another adult along for the ride, even if it was for a quick preschool drop-off, took away a bit of loneliness Elisa hadn't realized was there until now.

After they transferred the car seats to Sean's truck, he helped Lottie get buckled while Elisa buckled in Ava. He then opened the passenger door for Elisa.

"Ready to go?" he asked, trying to avoid staring too long at the professional woman walking around from the other side of the truck. While Sean was in his typical on-site gear—ragged jeans, a T-shirt and his Carhartt jacket—Elisa wore a trim-fitting blazer, long black pants and heels. She was stunning, and more than once, he caught a floral scent, either from her loose blond curls or a refreshing perfume.

"Thank you," she said, and quickly got in the truck, ignoring the hand he held out to help her up.

"No problem." He shut the door and jogged to the driver's side.

While he got situated behind the wheel, Elisa turned around, assuring Lottie everything was going to be fine. Lottie had her hands over her ears.

Sean also twisted toward the back seat, ignoring the beautiful woman just inches away. "Lottie, I need a little help with ol' Bess."

Lottie and Elisa exchanged questioning glances. In a more timid voice than usual, the little girl asked, "Who's Bess?"

Sean smiled wide and patted the dashboard. "This truck, of course. Does your car not have a name, *Auntie*?" He narrowed his eyes and cocked his head as he waited for Elisa to respond.

She feigned a frown. "Unfortunately, no. But isn't that neat that this truck has a name?" As she continued to keep her attention on Lottie, a golden ringlet slipped along her shoulder. Sean shoveled in breath and decided to turn to his steering wheel instead of allowing his senses to get the best of him. He wasn't expecting this simple favor to throw him well past friendly-neighborhood-landscaper status to knitting club hero. Not today. A pretty woman with a knock-out knack for design was great client material, nothing else.

He adjusted the rearview mirror. "Now, Lottie, have you ever seen someone blow up a balloon?"

Lottie nodded.

"Well, that's how ol' Bess gets started. With a few big breaths to wake her up. You think you can help me?"

"Me, too!" Ava exclaimed.

Elisa glanced at Sean with a knowing half smile.

He winked. Shouldn't have, because that was just what a knitting club hero should do, but it was a natural affirmation to someone catching on to his scheme—no matter if it was the pretty aunt or the preschooler herself. He diverted his attention to the rearview mirror again.

"Okay, Lottie and Ava—and Auntie, too." Did Elisa's blush just deepen? He locked eyes securely with the four-year-old through the rearview mirror. "On the count of three, we are going to blow straight toward the engine." He pointed to the front of the truck. "Okay, here we go." The two little girls gulped in air. He turned around again, stalling, amused by the girls' puffed-out cheeks. "Now, when she wakes up, it's going to be a bit rumbly, but that's normal. No need to be scared, right?"

Lottie nodded and kicked her legs against the seat. "Are you going to count, Mr. Sean?"

Elisa chuckled.

"Get your breath ready, too," he said to her. She faced forward, grinning wide. "One, two, three."

They all blew, and Sean turned the key in the ignition. Lottie and Ava cheered, and Elisa tossed her head back and laughed. Sean couldn't help but chuckle, too.

"That was easier than I thought it'd be," he muttered to Elisa.

Her brown eyes grew big, and she mouthed, "Same."

When they arrived at drop-off, two associate teachers helped the girls out of their seats. Jane chatted with Elisa at the passenger window.

"Bye, ol' Bess!" Lottie waved from the sidewalk.

Sean and Elisa waved in unison. As he pulled away from the school, Elisa's cell rang. She said it was her office, so she had to take it. Sean tried focusing on his clients' yards as he drove and not on Elisa's phone conversation out of courtesy. She hung up as they backed into her driveway. "You really helped so much this morning. They are going to want more rides in ol' Bess, I'm afraid."

Sean grinned and slung his elbow on the back of the bench seat. "Every Tuesday and Thursday afternoon."

"Truly, I am impressed with your quick thinking." Elisa placed her hand on his arm. Her eyebrows lifted with surprise. She scooted back and quickly opened the door. "Let me know if you have any questions while you work today."

"No problem. I am going to focus on the playset first." He opened his door and hopped out of the truck.

Elisa began toward the garage. "That sounds good. I have some drawings at the office I worked on last fall." She hesitated, then blew out a breath and fluttered her lashes. "Um, we'll get it figured out."

Sean approached her. "Are you okay?"

She weakly nodded. "Just haven't been back to the office since the week before New Year's. Going to be like starting all over again."

"I am sure they missed you." He rocked back on his heels.

Elisa rolled her eyes and sniggered. "Don't know about that." She searched the house before them. "But now—" Shaking her head gently, her pretty curls sliding along her pressed blazer, she said, "Those girls have become my everything, I guess. Can't believe how much I've learned that has nothing to do with work. You know, like when a straw is preferable to a sipper." She smiled. "Or the difference between a swirly slide and a plain ol' one."

"You forgot about starting a truck with a simple breath." He pushed his glasses on the bridge of his nose, hoping she didn't catch him staring too intently.

"Yes, that's especially useful."

Sean unlatched the tailgate of the truck and started unloading measuring tools. "I've been a partial caregiver since I was about fifteen years old. So, it's just second nature to me."

"Fifteen?"

"Yep. Mom left, and I became second-in-charge. But needless to say, it sure makes life full to have kids in your care. The great thing is, the longer you are apart, the sweeter the reunion is. So just be ready for lots of hugs tonight. Lottie probably gives very enthusiastic ones."

Elisa laughed. "Oh, yes, knock-off-your-feet bulldozing ones."

"Hey, I could use a bulldozer." Sean wagged his eyebrows toward the backyard.

Elisa just shook her head with a fading smile. "I better get going." Her heels clicked as she walked up the pavement to the garage's side door. She swiveled around. "Oh, preschool is over at three thirty. I told Jane our plan."

"Great. Blythe and I will be there." Sean pulled some sunglasses out of his shirt pocket and traded his spectacles. It was time to retire this brief knitting club hero gig, and finally become the landscape architect he'd planned to be.

Chapter Eight

Elisa's first day back at the office was so packed with meetings that not many people struck up conversations about anything other than work-related topics. She was relieved, but as she drove home and decompressed, she became unsettled. Shouldn't her work colleagues care to ask about her life at all? After the past few weeks in Rapid Falls, Elisa was half expecting a barrage of questions about life now. She must be tired. Caring about people asking questions was unlike her. Never before had she discussed much about her personal life. Why would anyone who'd only seen her on video calls the past two months want to ask personal questions of the rejected bride, the bereaved sister and the guardian of two little girls living in a sleepy small town?

By the time she pulled into the garage, the sun had slipped below the horizon. She hurried out of the car, gathering some takeout and her satchel, and climbed up the few steps into the mudroom. The house was quiet, but all the lights were on. Elisa's heels clicked along the wood floors. She set down the takeout on the kitchen island, plopped her satchel by the counter, then headed to the playroom. Her favorite guest bed sheet was draped over the play table with a couple kitchen chairs propping up the sheet's corners. Whispers skittered from underneath.

"Hey, girls, I'm home."

Giggles and hushing sounds followed.

"Come find us," Lottie shouted.

"I think she has," Blythe said, and appeared from under one side of the tent, static sending her blond hair in a frenzied array above her head. "Hi, Elisa."

Elisa bent down and peered past the sitter. "I take it you're having a good camping trip?"

Blythe crawled completely out from under the sheet and stood. "Actually, we were having a singing contest."

"A singing contest?"

Lottie and Ava scrambled out and ran up to Elisa, giving her the big hugs she was hoping for all day. If only Sean could see his prediction had come true.

"Blythe's mommy is famous." Lottie's hair was also wild with static.

Elisa smoothed it down while Blythe explained that her mom was an entertainer in Hawaii. "I showed the girls one of her performances, and we decided to have our own contest."

"Wow, your mom is in Hawaii?" Elisa recalled Sean mentioning their mother had left when he was fifteen.

Blythe pulled her hair into a ponytail. "Yep. She's a great singer. I listen to her a lot. Especially since we don't talk much." The thirteen-year-old's matter-of-fact admission that she didn't talk to her own mother took Elisa by surprise. "The girls were great. I think Ava might have been a little sad when we picked her up from preschool."

"Oh, really?" Elisa bent down and lifted Ava to her hip. "Did you have fun today?"

Ava nodded, then nestled her head in Elisa's neck.

"She missed you." Lottie was fixing the tent as it began to slip off the chair. "She cried at nap time. I heard her while we made crafts."

"Oh no." Elisa pulled away from Ava to look at her. "See, I came back. All done."

"It's night-night?" Ava asked with a furrowed brow, then pushed Elisa's face to look at the darkening window.

"Not yet. Soon, it will get lighter and lighter outside, and we'll have plenty of daylight after work." Elisa would try to leave a little earlier from Marion. Today, her last meeting had ended right at five o'clock. "I brought home fried chicken. Are you hungry?" She set Ava down and the girls ran to the kitchen.

"Blythe, I have enough for all of us now and for leftovers later. Want to join us?"

"Sure. I don't know if Sean's home yet. He headed to Waterloo for some more supplies." Blythe followed the girls. Elisa slipped off her heels, grabbed one of the kitchen chairs from the makeshift tent, careful to not destroy the creation, and carried the chair back to the kitchen so they would have enough seats. Blythe was already setting Ava in her booster seat at the table.

By the time Elisa made plates for her nieces, her stomach was growling. She said a quick prayer over the food, and they all began to eat.

"So, everything went okay today?" Elisa asked.

"Yes, the girls were great," Blythe said before taking a bite of mashed potatoes. "We had lots of fun. Oh, and Sean left a drawing for you on the living room console table. He measured the yard and cleared out the beds today."

"Great. Can't wait to look at the drawing." Elisa had emailed him the plans for the transition from the four-season room to the patio. "Girls, we're going to have to move your playroom." She scrunched her nose at their protesting. "I know. But my boss says so." Elisa knew the little girls didn't understand.

"That's the best part of working for yourself—you are your own boss." Blythe grinned wide. "At least, that's what Sean says."

"What do you want to do when you're older, Blythe?"

"Oh, I want to be a graphic designer." She beamed as if she'd found out she won an award. "I draw all the time. I am getting good at faces."

"I used to draw faces when I was around your age." Elisa thought back on her junior high notebooks with eyes and lips drawn all over the back pages. "We had to take a figure drawing class in college for my major. I have some books around here on sketching. I'll have to dig them out so you can take a look."

Blythe's face lit up again. "That would be great. I've been practicing using some old photographs of—" She dropped her gaze to her green beans and said softly, "My mom. But don't tell Sean." She rolled her eyes.

Elisa released a breathy laugh. She was curious about their mother's situation more and more, especially knowing how much of a rock Howard Peters had been in this town. Nobody mentioned his wife.

Elisa wouldn't ask any more questions tonight.

After so many meetings, she hardly had the energy to maintain a conversation. She longed for a quiet evening with a book and a fireplace, like her old habit after a busy day. But priority was her new role as a parent. The two little girls with crumbs on their cheeks would need a bath, a bedtime story and a whole bunch of snuggles.

Just before eight o'clock, Sean pulled up next to Elisa's car in his driveway. Phew. He had been worried about Blythe being home now that it was dark, but she hadn't answered his texts. He parked and headed over to Elisa's window while Blythe hopped out of the car. She dipped back inside the car to say goodbye to the girls, then greeted Sean before heading to the house. Elisa rolled her window down. Her eyes appeared weary as the interior lights faded off.

"How was your first day back?" he asked, leaning his forearm on the top of the car door.

"Good. Exhausting. I think I prefer emails to in-person meetings."

"Depends on what sugar and caffeine is available." Sean laughed. "So, did you get my drawing? As soon as you approve, we'll get the playset installed." He ducked his head down toward the back seat and said to the girls, "First things first. Right, Lottie? Playset coming up."

"Yippee!" Lottie squealed.

Ava just moaned a little with heavy eyelids, and she gathered her blanket to her chin.

Sean shifted to face Elisa again and quirked his mouth apologetically. "Oh, sorry, looks like bedtime's soon."

Elisa gave a weak smile. "Yes, I might skip bath time tonight."

"Every good parent does that once in a while." Sean stepped away from the window. "Look how well Blythe turned out. And Dad was a great bath skipper."

Elisa leaned her elbow on the opened window and peered up at him. Her eyes picked up whatever light they could find, and her pretty curls were now piled in a messy bun. "Blythe's such a great help. I noticed she even folded laundry."

"Sounds about right." Sean's usual wave of remorse for Dad missing out on his daughter's growing up dimmed his good mood. He swallowed away his emotion and stuck to business. "If you approve the drawings before work tomorrow, I can get started."

"Will do. I work at home on Wednesdays, so I can get it to you a little earlier since I don't have to drive anywhere but preschool."

"Sounds great." A wave of excitement knocked away old regret. "Can't wait to get to work."

Elisa sighed. "I wish tomorrow was the weekend. Today felt like a gazillion years. So yes, bath time is definitely going to be skipped."

"Get some rest." Sean waved goodbye, then strode toward the house. He watched her head down the street again. His creative energy had topped out today as he put together not only a plan for the playset and the transition space, but for the entire project. This had been a very good day for Sean Peters. At one last glance at the disappearing lights of his client's SUV, he had a hard time ignoring the fact that the day had started and ended with Elisa Hartley.

He'd better take care to focus purely on business, because he felt his pulse trip up on an old trap he'd cast off with Kylie—his overactive empathy. Of course, Sean would care for anyone who appeared exhausted as a new parent. He'd felt the same in the recent past. His compassion had nothing to do with an attractive woman walking a similar path as him, both personally and professionally.

He opened the front door. Blythe was cozied up on the couch with the remote.

She turned toward him and asked, "Did I ever act sad after Mom left?"

Sean shrugged. "I can't remember. But I know that Dad would have to take you to work with him sometimes. You wouldn't let him leave the house otherwise."

Blythe nodded. "That makes sense. Ava had a hard time today at preschool, according to Lottie. And she kept holding my hand no matter what we were doing." She laughed softly. "It was so sweet to see her face light up when she heard Elisa's voice."

"You've made a great impression on Elisa already," Sean said as he sat in the recliner, reaching for his book.

Blythe leaned her elbow on the couch arm and rested her cheek on her fist. "She's super nice. Talks to me like I am her friend more than a kid. She's just got that way about her."

Sean's jaw clenched involuntarily. Not too long ago, Blythe was saying similar things about Kylie. He knew he couldn't protect his sister from looking up to other women in her life—actually, he would love for Blythe to have a woman to ask questions that she didn't feel comfortable asking him. But he wanted to be sure she wasn't clinging to someone who would hurt her in the end.

"Elisa is pretty overwhelmed. You're a good helper for her, Blythe." *But don't get too attached,* he wanted to add. Although saying that might be a reminder that Blythe had little attachment to anyone but him and some of the older residents in town. His sister, now growing from girl to young woman, couldn't count on the one person who should be committed to her well-being. Mom reached out minimally, if at all. Blythe, on the other hand, seemed to keep her mom updated with texts often. The lack of responses irked Sean. Yet Mom had reached out to Dad and Sean for money since her health was declining. If Blythe only knew…

While Blythe thought Mom was busy with her wonderful career—Sean knew otherwise. Mom's career had been over long ago.

"Thanks, Sean. I can't wait to see the girls tomorrow." Blythe settled into watching a TV show, and Sean tried to read his book. He checked his heart once more. Yep, he was completely over being affected by his interaction with Elisa earlier. Whatever was welling up inside him after starting and finishing the day with his colleague—no, his employer—had everything to do with the effect of creativity abounding and the hope of saving his family business. That was it.

Chapter Nine

The next morning, the girls ate breakfast while Elisa finished an email to her new client. The woman was particular and expected quick responses to any question, having left a message at ten o'clock last night and then following up at seven this morning. But she was a respected entrepreneur, and Elisa was privileged to work for such a high-profile client.

"Ava doesn't go to school with me today?" Lottie asked as Elisa grabbed her backpack from the mudroom hook and tried to usher the girls out of the door.

"Nope. Only Tuesdays and Thursdays. Today's Wednesday." Ava wouldn't let go of Elisa's leg, so Elisa bent down and picked her up while handing Lottie the backpack.

"No school." Ava squirmed as Elisa tried to buckle her in. She started to whimper and pushed Elisa's hand away. "No."

"You aren't going, sweetie." Elisa tried to buckle her again, but Ava just cried. She kissed Ava's forehead and peered into her big chocolate eyes. "No school for Ava." The two-year-old's body relaxed. She gathered her blankie to her chest and lifted her elbows for Elisa to finish buckling her in.

At drop-off, Jane opened the door for Lottie and helped her to the sidewalk. "Good morning!"

Elisa grasped the passenger seat as she turned around to speak to Jane at the back door. "Hi, Jane. I was wondering if I could talk to Miss Bradley about yesterday."

"She's not here today since the two-year-olds are off. Is there anything I can help with?"

Ava was dozing in her seat, so Elisa lowered her voice. "It seems that Ava is terrified to come back to school. Lottie said she was crying yesterday. I just want to make sure nothing happened."

"That's too bad. I wonder if she has separation anxiety."

"But she did fine the first day of school."

"Yes, there's usually a honeymoon period with littles. Once they realize what's in store—a whole day without you—then there might be more resistance."

Elisa glanced at Ava, whose long eyelashes rested on her round cheeks as she softly snored.

"Okay, we'll have to pray for a good start tomorrow. Yesterday was a long one."

"It should get easier soon. Promise." Jane gave a reassuring smile, and they said goodbye.

When Elisa pulled up to the house, Sean was leaning on her porch column with two to-go cups. He held one up and nodded with bright eyes, signaling the coffee was for her. She waved back, ignoring the silly leap in her stomach at his thoughtfulness.

He met her in the garage as she carried Ava from the back seat to the door. The little girl was resting on Elisa's shoulder. Her head was heavy, a sign she was still sleeping.

"Let me get that," Sean whispered, rushing past them. He set the coffee on the workbench, then opened the door.

"Thank you," Elisa mouthed.

But keeping their voices low was futile. Little Ava popped her head up and said, "I not go to school."

Elisa giggled. "No, you aren't going. You're going to be my helper today." She lowered her to the floor. Instead of running into the house as usual, the little girl lifted her arms up and whimpered. Elisa picked her up while Sean headed back into the garage to grab the to-go cups. Ava held on with a tighter grip than before.

Sean joined them in the kitchen, adding a refreshing spicy scent to the air, warming Elisa more than a cup of coffee ever could.

"What did you bring me?" she asked.

"Sweet Lula's Latte. It's the best. Her barista is top-notch."

"Thanks for thinking of me." Her voice was small, but her gratitude was great. "So, are you ready to go over the plan? I have the drawing over here." She strode over to the kitchen table.

Sean joined her, setting her coffee in front of her while sipping his cup. "What are you thinking about the doors to the patio?" He splayed a hand on one side of the drawing and bent down to study her notes.

Elisa bounced Ava on her hip while Ava twirled Elisa's ponytail. "I think it would be great to have folding glass doors instead of sliding doors. They could go all the way—" She reached over to point to the plan, but Ava's blanket fell forward onto the drawing. "Here, sweet pea, let me set you down a sec—" Ava screeched and yanked Elisa's ponytail, gripping her tight. "Ouch. Ava!"

Sean reached out and uncurled Ava's fingers from Elisa's hair, speaking softly. "Ava, be gentle to your aunt."

Ava nestled her face in Elisa's neck, now wrapping both hands tightly around her shoulders. Elisa sat down. Surrendering the work talk, she explained, "She's probably got separation anxiety. But she and I are together, in the same house—I don't get it."

Sean pushed his chin up and shrugged his shoulders. He lowered to the chair across from her. "She wants to be right next to you all the time? That's probably it."

"She had a hard time at school yesterday. I thought she appeared fine when we dropped her off, didn't you?"

He nodded.

"I not go to school," Ava protested in a muffled voice.

Sean rubbed the back of his neck. "Blythe and I were just talking about this last night. When my m-o-m first left—" he cast a quick glance at Ava "—Blythe was super clingy to my father. Especially when he went out to the garage." He placed a gentle hand on Ava's back. "Maybe seeing us drive away yesterday…"

Elisa's throat tightened and unexpected tears sprang in her eyes. Charlie and Sylvia had driven away in his truck to go to a party that evening. She held Ava tighter. Maybe she was reminded of being left behind by her parents? "How old was Blythe?"

"Hmm, around Ava's age, actually."

Elisa frowned, then pressed her lips in Ava's brown curls. "It's okay, sweet pea. I won't leave you." But she couldn't promise that she would never leave her—she had to work. How would they get through tomorrow's drop-off? "How did Blythe grow out of it?"

He grimaced. "I don't really know. I was only in high school and probably in an adolescent brain fog." He chuckled. "But just keep being there for her. You're doing great." Sean placed his hand on hers and gave her a genuine smile.

"Thanks," she said, then slipped her hand away. His words were kind, but Elisa felt horrible because her first thought was about Ava disrupting her work-life balance.

"Grief is a beast." Sean sat back in the kitchen chair.

"You aren't exaggerating." Not only were Elisa and her nieces suffering the loss of Charlie and Sylvia, but Elisa grappled with a kind of grief whenever she remembered her dream of a life with Chad in this house.

Sean continued to sympathize. "It shows up unexpectedly…and it never really goes away. We just adapt. Ava will, too." He reached out a hand, not to Elisa this time, but to pat Ava's back again.

Would Elisa have ever considered this scenario for her life here in Rapid Falls—where the guy wasn't her husband, the girl wasn't her daughter, yet she felt completely enveloped in purpose and care?

Maybe she was adapting to the grief of her failed wedding. Funny, she considered the wedding more than the relationship. She squirmed at that as she realized that she was still the same reserved woman who'd been cast aside for a more adventurous affair.

Perhaps this reality was better than the dream family. At least she didn't have to fulfill someone else's dream-girl shoes right now. She could hardly figure out what kind of shoes she could fit in—fast-and-ready career heels or slow-and-steady guardian sneakers. Her phone dinged with three email notifications in a row.

"I guess I'm going to have to squeeze in a whole bunch of work during nap time," she conceded, and took a sip of her latte for the first time. Her eyes widened. "Wow, that's good."

Sean dipped his chin with pride. "The best. Maybe that's how my dad got through it. Sweet Lula's has a way of making everything a little easier to deal with. Just one sweet treat at a time."

Elisa grinned and took another sip. "I guess I would rather count sweet treats than emails."

Sean rolled up the plan. "I am going to look at the four-season room to see about the flooring. I won't be doing that myself. The flooring guy is heading here sometime this afternoon."

"Sure thing." Elisa led the way. "I meant to get started on moving the toys last night."

Sean laid the plan in the corner and lifted a toy bin. "No worries. I can help with that."

"Are you sure?"

"Definitely." There were only a few bins, a small bookcase, and a kid-size table and chairs. "Where do you want them to go?"

"I guess we'll just make a corner in the living room for now. Will be interesting to see how I can get this place immaculate for a tour." Elisa blew a strand of hair from her face in exasperation.

Sean noticed stress in her brow and her turned-down mouth. A familiar look. Perhaps similar to the night she'd pulled up to the house. He nudged her with an elbow. "Hey, one sweet treat at a time, remember?" She relaxed and smiled only with her eyes, enchanting and bright. His gaze slipped to her lips. Searching for a smile? Or something else? His own lips parted.

Elisa's expression shifted from gratitude to surprise.

Sean looked away. They both stepped back from each other. He cleared his throat and continued through the living room to the corner by the window.

Elisa turned on the TV and set Ava on the couch with her blankie. "You know, I can do this myself, Sean."

"It's no problem—"

"See, Ava's fine. Don't worry about it. I've got the inside of the house taken care of." She gave a tight smile, then swiveled around and gathered up another bin. "Do you mind showing yourself out? I assume you're heading out back." So, this was her business-professional voice. Completely matter-of-fact, emotionless.

"Sure thing. See you later." He shoved a hand in his pocket, patted Ava on the head as he passed, grabbed the plan and headed out back.

Embarrassment filled his chest. He didn't mean to be so enraptured by the woman—and any other day, he would have probably resisted sending any signals of interest. His admiration for Elisa's strength and talent was not the same as affection, even if his response appeared that way. Sitting with Elisa, discussing ways to care for those they loved, had been a change from the small-town happenings he usually chatted about with neighbors and lifelong friends. Elisa was new and interesting. He'd been thrown off guard, that was all.

Sean wanted to march back in there and apologize for making it awkward. He would explain that she was becoming a friend, and he'd reacted involuntarily to a tender moment. Maybe she would agree, admitting she felt the same way about being friends. And maybe they would continue to meet for lattes and discuss life aside from work, because who wouldn't want to start their day with heartfelt conversation?

Sean rolled his eyes at himself.

All he needed right now was to work. Because the most important thing in his life was not playing advisor to a new neighbor—attractive as she was—but salvaging his family business so he could lay a solid foundation for his sister and their future. Last time he depended on a woman to assist in securing that foundation, his sister was left devastated, and Sean had invested way too much of his happiness in one person.

He glimpsed Elisa pacing through the window, her cell phone to her ear. Realization twisted his insides. The distressed look she had given earlier wasn't from her first night in Rapid Falls, but the same expression he'd seen from his rearview mirror long ago. Heat swarmed his face. She had been a stranger then. Now she was in his life every day, but too much time had passed for Sean to mention the ride in his dad's Mustang. At least, he thought so.

This last encounter with Elisa was a subtle misstep. Sharing that he'd been sole witness to her meltdown, understandable as it was, after all this time, would no doubt humiliate Elisa and end any relationship—business or otherwise—between them. Most importantly, Elisa was his much-needed employer. Sean shifted his focus to this project like his life depended on it. Actually, his professional life did depend on it. He headed through the gate to get started.

Chapter Ten

Elisa ended the call with her new client, trying to keep Ava from knocking the phone out of her hand. Her niece had started begging for her attention toward the end of the conversation. And while Elisa attempted to wrap things up when Ava grew louder, Elisa could not get through to her client that an impromptu run to the woman's house, an hour away, was not feasible right now. Finally, her client had agreed to an actual scheduled meeting right before Ava pulled Elisa's sweater, making her double over to be sure she didn't stretch it.

"Ava, you may not do that." She carefully unclasped Ava's fingers like Sean had when the toddler clutched at Elisa's ponytail. She crouched down and looked at the toddler straight on. "You need to say, 'Excuse me,' and wait until I can help you."

"'Scuse me." She grabbed at Elisa's sweater again.

A mixture of amusement and agitation erupted in a groan from Elisa as she removed Ava's hand again. Ava appeared startled, and her bottom lip stuck out. Maybe Elisa's frustration was more obvious than she realized. As uncertainty filled Ava's face, Elisa's usual feeling of inadequacy pressed heavily on her spirit.

"You aren't in trouble, Ava. Just use your words." Elisa rubbed the back of Ava's tiny knuckles with her thumb.

"Milk, please?" Ava's voice was meek.

"Of course. Thanks for asking nicely." Elisa stood and went to the kitchen. Tiny footsteps toddled behind her. She gave Ava a sippy of milk. "Let's try and take a nap, Ava."

"Nooo," she protested, with the sippy cup in her mouth.

"Yesss." Elisa reached down and took her hand. They went up the stairs carefully. Picking her up would be quicker, but last time Elisa had spoken on the phone with Mom, she had suggested Ava needed to get used to climbing the stairs. If only Mom could be here to coach Elisa all the time.

Surprisingly, Ava lay down in her bed without any fuss, her eyes heavy as she finished her milk. Elisa took the cup, closed the bedroom door, then quietly moved through the house so she could get to her computer. Okay, this was working exactly how she'd planned. The minutes ticked by with contentedness. Her niece was safe and sound, and she'd be able to send dates to her client so promptly after ending their call.

Elisa was in a groove when shouts and a loud truck engine sounded from the backyard simultaneously with Ava's snores through the baby monitor. Elisa froze, fluttered her lashes and waited.

Not. One. Peep. Please.

She needed to get this work done. *This* needed to work if she was going to keep Ava with her during her work-at-home days. The sound of lumber clattering sent Elisa's jaw into vise mode. Then Ava began to whimper.

Elisa swiveled out of her chair with the baby monitor in her hand, praying that Ava would fall back asleep. She hurried through the house and out the back door. A truck unloaded what appeared to be parts to the playset. Sean was standing with a crew member, discussing the plan that was sprawled out on an old patio table. He wore sunglasses, a pencil behind his ear and a boyish grin to top off his appearance of being completely in his element.

Whatever had passed between them earlier— first, a suspicion that Sean considered her lips more than her words in the moment, followed quickly by a leap in her chest—well, whatever that was, thinned into nothingness like the threadbare clouds on this sunny spring day.

Sean looked over at her as she neared. His grin broadened, then dropped. Elisa was never good at pretending to be okay when she was this worked up. A flaw that made her so thankful for the quick thinking of that guy who'd driven her away from her wedding before the guests found out she'd been stood up. He had given her as much privacy to grieve as a back seat could offer.

Sean met her on the other side of the patio. "Hey, there." He regarded the pile of wood behind him. "We have all the parts for the playset. Going to get started right away."

"Great."

He pulled off the sunglasses and raised an eyebrow. "Anything wrong with this plan?"

Elisa let out a heavy breath and crossed her arms. "So, remember how I told you that I wasn't ready for this type of disruption among the other things going on right now?"

"Uh, yeah?"

Ava's whimper turned into a wail of "Auntie!"

Elisa held up the monitor. "Nap time was a very important thing going on right now."

"Oh, man, I am sorry." Sean rubbed the back of his neck. Pure remorse softened his brow. "So, does she typically nap at this time? I can keep it in mind from here on out."

Ava's voice grew louder.

Elisa rolled her eyes and began to walk away, explaining, "I guess this is the normal nap time. But if I've learned anything about parenthood, I can't guarantee anything." She loped back into the house to get Ava, resorting to working on the final touches in the girls' bedrooms until Blythe arrived.

For a woman who'd carefully worked according to her schedule, preserving her resources at all costs—both emotion-wise and peace-and-quiet-wise—Elisa was now fighting to maintain a bare minimum of control. She prayed for just a little bit more than minimum—or at least to have the assuredness that Sean seemed to emanate. The man was practically glowing over the backyard plans.

Could Elisa Hartley really consider parenthood being in her element at all? Would she ever be the type of parent the girls needed—self-assured, like Sean?

That afternoon, Elisa pulled into the driveway from preschool pickup right as Blythe was heading to the front door. Blythe met them in the garage and helped the girls out of their seats.

Elisa set an alarm on her phone. She couldn't miss her four o'clock conference call. "I am going to be in my room for the rest of the afternoon." She grabbed some snacks for the girls and pulled out a chair for Lottie. "Oh, there are those books I mentioned, Blythe." She motioned to the stack at the center of the table.

"Yay. I am excited to look at them." Blythe sat down with Ava on her lap and began to flip through the first one. Elisa was thankful that Ava didn't shy away from the babysitter.

"Your brother might even have that book. It's about sketching landscapes."

Blythe stopped and studied a page. "Look, Lottie, this is where my mom lives." She turned the book around. Elisa peered over. Palm trees and seascape. Blythe looked up at her. "I really hope to save and go visit her one day." For the first time since Elisa met Blythe, her brightness dulled to melancholy.

Elisa lowered in the seat next to her. "How often does she come here?"

Blythe pressed her mouth into a dismissive smile, slid her gaze to the book and shook her head. "She's only been here twice that I remember. Once, when my grandpa died. She came for the funeral. I was Lottie's age."

Lottie straightened. Her mouth was filled with Goldfish crackers, but she managed to say, "I'm four." Elisa nodded and reminded her to not talk with a mouthful.

Blythe continued, "Yep. Four. And then when I was ten. Right before Kylie left." A full-on storm crossed Blythe's face.

"Kylie?"

"Sean's ex-girlfriend. She was really nice. I thought she'd stay forever."

Elisa tripped up on the word *forever*. She knew the feeling that obviously crossed Blythe's face. Still grappling with the disappointment that obliterated what was thought to be a sure ever-after.

Blythe let out a short laugh and rolled her blue eyes. "Silly me. Nobody stays around here that's cool."

Elisa feigned offense by dropping her jaw and narrowing her eyes. "What about the cool people who choose to move to Rapid Falls?" She smiled in Lottie's direction.

"We live in Rapid Falls!" Lottie exclaimed.

Blythe giggled. "Mom says it's not for everyone. But I love that it's good for you guys." She tickled Ava, who giggled as she popped a cracker in her mouth. Elisa studied Blythe. The girl stared hard at the page as she traced the palm tree with her finger.

Elisa had grown up with both parents in her life but understood the sorrow of separation between a parent and a child. Her brother had chosen to keep his distance from Dad all of Elisa's life. No matter how many times they actually spoke, it never seemed enough for her dad.

Elisa couldn't imagine a little girl being satisfied with such distance from her mom. Sean walked by the kitchen window out back. He was filling some pretty giant shoes—not just those of the late Howard Peters, whom everyone loved—but stepping in as two parents to this amazing teen. Elisa was doing the same for her nieces.

She prayed thanksgiving for being acquainted with Sean's example of walking in several pairs of shoes at once.

Blythe's cloudy countenance disappeared, and she asked, "So, you think if I practice sketching, it will help with graphic design?"

"Absolutely," Elisa affirmed with a firm tap on the table, and stood. "I'd love to sit here and sketch with you, but I better get to my phone call."

Blythe unzipped her backpack in the chair next to her and asked Lottie, "Want to draw pictures?"

"Yes!" Lottie's delight matched her babysitter's enthusiasm, and the domino effect expelled Ava's signature squeal.

Elisa warmed and made her way upstairs, closing her door with a quiet thud. But as she settled at her computer, she kind of wished she could have stayed downstairs. Sitting with Blythe and the girls brought about a sense of purpose—not in doing anything in particular, but in being there, listening and helping direct a little hope for someone else.

Sean tried to focus on the work of prepping the area for the playset, but uneasiness traveled its way up his spine. Earlier, he'd noticed Blythe sitting at Elisa's kitchen table, and his sister seemed completely enthralled in conversation. Of course, with a spunky teen like Blythe, most conversations were enthralling. Sean chuckled at the thought. But his own humor wasn't enough to shake the déjà vu that struck him hard, like he'd walked straight into that kitchen window. The last time he'd seen Blythe engaged in girl talk with an adult was when Kylie was here that summer three years ago. But the happy memory of that season was tainted by the rejection not long after.

Was Blythe maturing enough to not depend so much on attention she never got from a mom? Only lately had they found a new normal without Dad around. Maybe it was a good thing that Elisa had hired Blythe. Knowing how Elisa was protective of her own time, Sean might not need to worry about Blythe getting too attached.

Sean reasoned his discomfort away and focused on the project. It was coming along nicely.

"Hey, there, Sean," Ed Benton, the flooring guy, boomed as he walked across the patio slab, head down, observing its poor condition. "Can't wait to get rid of this. So, what are you thinking?"

They shook hands, then went over the outdoor space. Sean opened the sliding door into the four-season room. He explained the concept of bringing the flagstone into both spaces, and how they would manage the different elevations.

"I think we can make this work real nice." Ed took out his tape measure as he looked around the room. "I was just on a project for Innovations—that's the firm the owner works for, right?"

Sean nodded as he peeked in the kitchen. Blythe and the girls were coloring.

Ed lowered his voice and said, "This is not their typical kind of residence. You should see the square footage on the one outside of Des Moines." Ed whistled and began to measure. "I believe you struck gold just being associated with that firm, Sean."

"That's the hope."

"Hey, Sean!" Blythe waved, then Lottie scrambled down from her chair and ran up to him.

"Is my playset ready?"

"Not yet." Sean crouched down. "But don't worry, you'll be all set for spring break next week." Ava toddled over and Blythe followed close behind her.

Lottie addressed Ed, who was measuring the width of the room. "Mister, I know how to use that. My daddy taught me." She pointed at the measuring tape.

Ed chuckled. "How many inches in a foot?" He held the tape, pointing to the twelve-inch mark.

Lottie patted her finger on her lip as she examined the number. Her eyes lit up, and she declared, "Twelve!"

"Impressive. Are you looking for a job? I could use a good assistant."

Elisa appeared from the living room. "Uh, what's going on here?" She leaned on the doorjamb with her arms crossed. Sean couldn't tell if she was casual or suspicious. Last time they stood in this room, she'd transformed from friendly to businesslike in a matter of seconds. Seemed she was still in businesslike mode as she tapped her pencil on her arm, appearing completely unamused.

"This is Ed Benton, the flooring guy. We're just talking about the transition space," Sean explained. "And Lottie is being offered a job." He winked at Lottie.

"Oh, good," Elisa replied, and everyone looked her way. She faintly laughed. "Not about Lottie—you are much too young—but about the space." She crossed over to Ed. "The transition from indoor to outdoor is the most crucial part of the project." Elisa began to discuss details.

Lottie lost interest quickly, grabbed Sean's hand and tugged him toward the kitchen. "Mr. Sean, you need to see what Blythie drew."

"Blyth*ie*?" He cocked an eyebrow to his sister.

"That's what they call me." She grinned.

"Look!" Lottie ran over and grabbed a sheet of paper and held it up. "Hawaii!"

"Wow, that's pretty good, Blythe," Sean exclaimed, pushing his glasses up.

"Yes, that's great," Elisa affirmed over Sean's shoulder. Sean stepped aside. "Keep up the practice, Blythe."

"She's going to make posters for her mommy," Lottie informed everyone, then handed Blythe the drawing and climbed up in her chair.

Blythe picked up Ava and sat in her chair without looking at Sean. He didn't want her to feel weird around him when it came to talking about Mom, and he forced his jaw to stop clenching. But he had a hard time with Blythe's expectations of any future with their mother.

Before he could think of something to say, Elisa took over the awkward silence. "I am sure she gets her creative talent from the landscape architect in her life." The businesslike demeanor seemed to vanish. Her eyes shone bright at him. "If we pooled our old studio tools and textbooks together for Blythe, she'll be fully prepared for graphic design school."

Blythe seemed delighted and focused on the paper in front of her. He had no idea she was interested in design school. Why hadn't she told him? Maybe because it had something to do with a grand marketing scheme for their mom?

Sean sighed and began to return to work but caught Elisa's warm gaze. Guess her business hours were ending. But the slight lift of her chin with a sympathetic smile made him suspect she had been part of the conversation about their mom needing posters. What else had Blythe shared?

Chapter Eleven

The next day, Elisa parked at the preschool instead of going through the pickup line. As soon as she had placed Ava's bag in the car this morning, Ava had begun to protest school. She was crying by the time they pulled into the parking lot.

When Elisa got out of the car, her stiletto heel caught in a pothole she hadn't noticed. She stumbled forward, and her heel snapped. Elisa moaned. She'd have to go change her shoes before heading to Innovations. Right now, she couldn't focus on anything except Ava's hearty cry. "Mama."

"Hey, Ava, it's okay." Elisa unbuckled her. Tears streamed down the two-year-old's face. Lottie seemed affected, too—her brown eyes wide and her little brow in folds. Elisa spoke softly, "You have fun at school. Remember the blocks center?" Ava's legs encircled Elisa's waist desperately and tightly, as if they were standing on the edge of a cliff, not on the flat parking lot surface. Her wet face pressed on Elisa's shoulder. Elisa pushed away the thought of not only needing to go home and change shoes but her silk blouse as well. Ava's well-being was more important than her outfit. She squeezed the girl in a big hug, then pulled away to look at her.

"How about you go to school and I go to work and—"

"Good morning, ladies," Jane greeted as she approached. "Can I help get Lottie for you?"

Elisa tossed a grateful look over Ava's tiny pigtails now pressed against her jaw. "That would be great." She kissed Ava's forehead and continued to calm her. "Why don't we have a picnic for dinner?"

Ava popped her head up, sniffling. "With blankie?"

"Sure."

Elisa's own emotions warred within her. Ava's nose and eyes were red, and her cheeks flushed. Her distressed features flung Elisa back to when she and her parents had first cared for the girls after the accident. Because Charlie had hardly visited his father, her parents were practically strangers to the girls. Tears were frequent. And Ava would call for her mama most nights. But by the time they left for Rapid Falls, the girls had grown attached to their grandparents—whimpering as they drove away from Grangewood.

Today, Ava seemed to calm once Elisa walked her to the doors. Elisa left her in Jane's arms, praying for a good day on the drive home.

After she changed, Elisa detoured from her usual route out of town and onto Main Street instead. She parked and hurried to Sweet Lula's—now wearing ballet flats instead of heels. Only a few people sat at the tables, but there was a line along the counter. At the back of the shop, Lula was carefully transferring powdered cookies from a tray to the display case, one cookie at a time. Her rolling accent carried across the room as she chatted with a customer.

After a few minutes of waiting, Elisa grew anxious that she was going to be late to her first meeting. Maybe a drive-through in the city would be a better option? She turned to go and nearly crashed into Sean.

"Oh, hey, there." She refrained from the step she was going to take since he was already so close.

Sean glanced at her loosely curled hair. "I was just about to say hi. I thought it was you." He remained steady, emanating friendliness. His refreshing, spicy scent competed with the coffeehouse aroma.

"Yep, it's me. Just trying to get this day in gear."

After the morning she'd had, she wanted to drive to her parents' instead of work. But somehow, the sight of Sean Peters had the same effect on her as curling up on her mom's couch with a book and some peace. The man she'd seen nearly every day this past week was comfort and understanding wrapped up in the most handsome form. Tension rolled off her shoulders, and the space between them didn't seem to be too small, but just shy of close enough.

Whoa. She needed to step back. How had they found themselves in a similar predicament after that incident in her living room?

Being new in Rapid Falls had tapped into a weakness she'd longed to cast off the day she left her wedding—trusting someone else to be what she needed. Sure, comfort and understanding were nice perks, but Elisa wasn't about to seek them out from her hired landscape architect, debonair as he was. She smiled at the knitting club's classic word for Sean Peters slipping into her thoughts.

"Do I amuse you?" He mirrored her smile, but his was no doubt much more enticing than hers.

Elisa, stop it.

"No, I was just thinking about the last time we were here with our local knitting ladies."

He pushed his spectacles up and shook his head. "Yes, if we didn't know each other, this near run-in today would be the meet-cute of the month for them."

And her heart maybe skipped a little. "I gotta go. It's been a day already, and this line is taking a while—"

Sean waved his hand, signaling behind her. "You're next."

She spun around and moved toward the counter, speaking over her shoulder, "Good. It's been a hectic morning, and the best latte ever was calling my name."

"Ah, so you liked it?" He was now almost beside her and playfully bumped her shoulder with his arm, sending a fleet of butterflies in her tummy. "And who do you have to thank for that?" He narrowed his eyes, in an almost smoldering way.

Oh, Elisa. Coffee is definitely needed to wake up to reality.

How far away would she need to get from this guy to remain her usual independent, introverted self?

"Just kidding. But I am sorry you had a hard start today." Sean straightened and crossed his arms over his chest. Did she give a standoffish vibe just now? Well, she should. Flirty banter did not fit in Elisa Hartley's job description as either a guardian to two little girls or as an interior designer.

"Thanks." Elisa approached the counter and

ordered from a perky barista who must have had her fair share of coffee. She stepped over to the end of the counter to wait for her drink while Sean ordered. By the time Elisa's latte was ready, her anxiety had kicked in again. Sean was right behind her as she wove back through the shop.

"Let me get that for you," he offered, racing beside her to hold open the door.

"Thank you." She stepped onto the sunny sidewalk and strode to her car. But a large utility truck was blocking her from backing out of her space. Her heart began to race as she considered the very real possibility of missing her first meeting altogether.

"Uh, wonder how long this guy's going to be here?" She unlocked her car with the key fob, hoping the beep would hint to the truck driver that he needed to move.

"Looks like Sally's boutique is having an issue." Sean placed his coffee on top of his truck cab just a couple spots from Elisa's. "Come on, let's see what's going on. We can ask the utility guy to move for you also." He began to cross the street, then turned around, walking backward. "Well, are you coming?"

"I really don't have time for this." Elisa blew a curl from her nose and huffed as she reluctantly followed Sean.

* * *

The boutique's French door was propped open. A man dressed in uniform coveralls passed through with a bucket full of drywall pieces. Sean had a feeling he knew exactly what must've happened. The old pipes in the shop had made a mess of poor Sally's Iowa collectibles and home decor pieces earlier, too.

Sally appeared at the doorway, brushing her gray-blond bangs to the side of her penciled-in eyebrows. "Water line disaster, Sean. Can you believe it?" The jovial laugh lines around her eyes and corners of her mouth were weighed down with worry. Sean squeezed her shoulder. "I just fixed it last summer. Can't afford to close down again. Business is just getting going after the rough winter."

Sean stepped back to introduce the two women. "Hey, Elisa, this is Sally Grover. Sally, Elisa Hartley."

"Oh, you bought the Victorian on Birch?"

"Yes, that's me." Elisa reached out and shook Sally's hand. The work truck's reversing sensors began to beep. "I am sorry to go, but I have to get to work."

"No worries. I've been meaning to give you a welcome gift. I'm also on the town's hospitality committee. Couldn't make the knitting club welcome." Sally smiled and folded her arms across her interesting poncho-type covering. She was as eclectic as her shop. Her many rings clinked against her bangles.

Elisa stopped at the curb, seeming genuinely flattered. Somehow, the way her cheeks flushed and the brightness of her brown eyes struck Sean right in the center of his chest. He may have seen the gamut of Elisa Hartley's reactions from the day of her wedding to this greeting from the friendliest woman in Rapid Falls. Sean would rather fight his involuntary reactions to Elisa than see her upset again.

"Thank you. I feel very welcomed around here. But I really must go." She gave a small wave to Sean, then rushed across the street.

"She's pretty, don't you think?" Sally leaned against the door. Her clinking jewelry made a signature sound.

Sean narrowed his eyes at her. "Don't start with your knitting club shenanigans, Mrs. Grover."

"Just stating the truth and asking your opinion."

Sean laughed as the worker passed between them and into the shop. "I think you have more important business than discussing the attractiveness of our newest resident. Besides, you remember the last time a pretty girl was in town?" He felt his smile fade, frustrated that he'd even brought his ex into the conversation, especially to Sally. Sally had hired Kylie as an apprentice.

Kylie had majored in entrepreneurship, hoping to own a store one day. Just like Blythe had grown attached to Sean's girlfriend, Sally had also come to love Kylie like a daughter.

"Have you talked to Kylie at all?" she asked.

"Nope. Why would I?"

Sally sighed and lifted her shoulders. "I don't know. If she reached out to you, then maybe there'd be hope for her to return my messages, too."

A cloud of disappointment hovered over them both, and guilt disrupted Sean's good mood for the day. He'd lost so much trust in his own discernment, not only because Kylie had broken his heart, but because she'd left holes in the hearts of two people he cared about. Actually, three. Dad had treated Kylie like a future daughter-in-law.

Sean's stomach soured. Kylie had said she'd felt suffocated by Sean's small-town ambitions—or what was it she'd said? *Obligations.* She didn't understand the importance of family and sacrifice, in the end.

Elisa's SUV passed by, and she waved through the window. Elisa was in the thick of sorting through family and sacrifice right now. The best thing Sean could do—regardless of the knitting club's meddlings—was create a backyard retreat for the girls and Elisa while making sure he didn't complicate life for anyone else.

Chapter Twelve

Elisa's mother's comforting voice came through the car's speaker. Elisa had explained Ava's fit this morning, her heel breaking and the car being blocked in.

"I just keep thinking, my commute from Rapid Falls is no different than commuting from you all. I don't know that having this new family home is any more beneficial than plan B."

"I understand, honey. You know you all are always welcome to plan B—our upstairs is ready and never gets used now that you all are—" Mom sounded like she was going to say something but stopped herself.

"What? What were you going to say?"

"I just think you need to give living there a little more time. You don't want to regret anything."

"It's just a house, Mom."

"But it sounds like you are connecting to the town, too."

"I guess. It does feel refreshing not to be defined as the woman who practically got stood up at the altar." Elisa half laughed and rolled her eyes as the Iowa countryside sped by. Rolling hills, budding trees and bare fields ready for planting.

"If you did move to Grangewood, nobody will think of you that way. Life moves along for everyone. It's been almost four months." She seemed to hesitate again. Elisa waited, craving the peace her mother often provided in times of distress. "You haven't heard anything, have you? I mean, from Chad?"

Elisa gripped the steering wheel tighter, and her voice came out thin and sharp. "Nope. Not since the week he got back from the Caribbean."

"Sorry, I shouldn't have said anything. I am so proud of you, Lees. You're giving those girls a place to grow."

"Attempting to." Although Elisa couldn't ignore the fact that she wasn't alone in offering the girls that growing place. Sean immediately came to mind, full of advice, building the playset, creating an outdoor space for all of them. Elisa hadn't planned on such a partnership with her landscape guy. "You're right, Mom. I need to give it time. But I would love for you all to plan a trip here soon."

"Definitely. Dad's thinking about taking some time off around Easter. Would love to be with the girls on Easter morning." She chuckled. "And you, of course."

"That sounds great." Elisa shoveled in air, the faint coffee aroma waking her to the reality that the best latte had hardly been sipped. They wrapped up the conversation and said goodbye. She took a sip of her latte and savored the warmth.

Sean Peters popped in her mind again, having been the first person to introduce her to this drink. What was it about that guy that rivaled the same peace her mother so consistently provided Elisa? Sean was empathetic and wise. Maybe that was it—Sean was a resource for Elisa's new season of parenthood. But she had to admit, his company had a lot to do with the peace, too.

Elisa was in a strange balance. At any moment, she'd tip the scales too far and fall into... what? Constantly frazzled guardian mode or depending too much on those around her? Hmm, surely there was a third option—one that didn't deplete her energy nor made her heart skip a beat at the thought of one particular guy she was running into every day.

Elisa needed to focus on the truth. She was

tiptoeing along the scales for a reason—first, she was recovering from trusting her heart to someone else, losing confidence in herself. And second, two little girls needed her to be someone completely different than who she'd been. Her nieces weren't the only ones needing a place to grow.

That evening, Elisa tucked the girls in bed, thankful that Ava had had a decent day. Jane had said she wouldn't go down at nap time, so she'd been Jane's helper around the preschool instead. Elisa admired the grace Jane exuded, and her example was somehow comforting. Modifying the plan didn't mean failure when kids were involved; it just meant getting creative on how to continue to be productive.

Elisa needed the reminder the next day when she procrastinated nap time, hoping Sean's crew would soon finish demolishing the old concrete patio. Finally, after getting a few emails out while Ava watched some cartoons, Elisa bundled up the little girl and carried her upstairs, regardless of the constant ruckus outside.

"Ugh, it's so loud," Elisa muttered to herself as she cranked up the white-noise machine in Ava's room. Lapping waves didn't quite mask the banging destruction, but it was all Elisa could do. "Come on, baby girl, Auntie needs to get on a video call."

Ava whimpered but seemed tired enough. She didn't resist lying down with her blankie.

Quickly, Elisa headed to her room, which was closer to the noise, but thankfully, she could use her headphones for the meeting. As she logged in, the steady slug of a sledgehammer shook her blinds. At least it was a consistent beat. She rolled her eyes and continued to get ready for her meeting.

As soon as Gerard started the conversation with the group, Elisa noticed that the baby monitor light was pulsing full blast. Maybe Ava would fuss a bit, then fall asleep. However, unease crawled along Elisa's spine as her head filled with images of Ava climbing out of her crib and flipping onto the hardwood floor. Finally, Elisa sent her boss a private message saying she'd be right back, then pulled off her headphones and ran down the hall.

Ava was hysterical. She gripped the rails of the crib, sucking in breath and tears, her chest heaving. Had something startled her more than the noise outside? Elisa had never seen her like this. After picking her up, Elisa tried to soothe her. The toddler's little breaths stuttered, shaking against Elisa's body.

"You can rest in my bed while I work." When

they got to Elisa's room, the demolition outside grew exceptionally loud. Ava's entire body stiffened. She began to cry again.

Elisa messaged Gerard again. She would have to get notes after the meeting. This wasn't working. Since Gerard wanted her backyard project to happen for the Tour of Remodeled Homes, Elisa hoped he'd understand the project pulling her away from other meetings. Of course, being a care provider wasn't necessarily a task under her job description at work, but Elisa felt ill-equipped to balance her responsibilities right now.

They headed downstairs, her frustration growing with each step. Hadn't she told Sean that they would be home on Fridays? Why did he pick today to do the loudest work?

The stroller was visible through the window on the front porch. A walk was just what Elisa needed, and probably Ava, too. Be creative, just like Jane. Maybe Elisa could call into the meeting while they walked. She'd try anything.

"Let's go on an adventure, Ava," Elisa said. Ava gripped tighter when Elisa opened the door. The backyard commotion was all the more evident, and Ava began to melt down again.

Sean appeared from around the corner and took the porch steps two at a time. He slid his sunglasses on top of his short light brown hair.

Elisa had hardly seen him without his usual glasses. His hazel eyes captured all shades of gold from the daylight.

Sean noticed Ava's distress and wiped a tear from her cheek. "Hey, sweet girl," he said softly. "Everything okay?"

"The noise is unbearable." Elisa didn't look at him and kept her gaze on Ava.

Sean stepped back and groaned. "Oh no. I'm sorry about that. But you should see the progress. Already starting to look better."

Elisa tried to swallow a biting remark about an apology not being good enough at this point. She managed a tight smile and tried to pry Ava off her torso to strap her in the stroller. "I am trying to salvage a phone meeting that is going on as we speak. I'll call in as we walk. Come on, Ava."

Sean crouched down next to the stroller and pulled off some protective headphones from around his neck. "Hey, Ava. Try these. They have hero powers." He carefully placed them on her head, dodging her protesting kicks.

As soon as the headphones were over her ears, she froze. Her brown eyes rounded, and she smiled at Sean. "The bad guys are all gone," she bellowed from her tiny, worked-up lungs.

Sean tossed his head back with a hearty laugh. Elisa couldn't help but grin, shaking her head with the last ounce of exasperation. "You know, if I had suggested those headphones, I have a feeling they'd have been thrown across the room." Elisa finished buckling Ava into the stroller.

Sean rose. "Again, I am sorry for the noise. They were supposed to come yesterday. But you know how unpredictable crew schedules can be."

Elisa straightened and rolled her shoulders.

"I wanted to ask if you'd be around this afternoon to check out the flagstone when it's delivered?" He winced as if he were asking her to set up Ava's crib in the middle of the crushed-up patio.

"I certainly hope this walk doesn't take us into the afternoon." She squeezed the bridge of her nose, trying to breathe away the tension building inside.

"Next week will be better with Blythe helping." Sean lifted his hand as if he was going to squeeze her shoulder, but it landed on the stroller's handle instead.

Elisa gave him a quizzical look. "I can't even think about next week until I get my work done today."

"At least it will be spring break. Blythe will entertain the girls so you can work uninterrupted." He dipped his head down and said to Ava, "And the playset will be ready."

Ava's eyelids were heavy.

"Those headphones are as big as her cheeks. She probably can't hear you." Elisa stepped behind the stroller handle. "But yes, having Blythe here all day will be very helpful." She pulled her hair back with a hair tie. "Mind helping me down the steps?"

"Sure." He lifted one end of the stroller and guided it down, stepping backward, while Elisa lifted from the handle. Sean huffed as he set the stroller on the walkway to the driveway. He stuck his hands in his back pockets and said, "Parenting isn't for the faint of heart, is it? I remember my mom's sleepless nights when Blythe was a baby." He hesitated, opened his mouth to speak then seemed to think better of it.

"When did your parents get divorced?"

"Divorced?" Sean faintly sneered. "They never divorced. Mom just left. Dad held on to the hope that she'd stay for good each random time she showed up. She's not like you, Elisa." He placed his hand on hers. "You are putting these girls first, doing the good but hard thing. My mom decided her dream was more important than her family." He slid his hand away, sending goose bumps across Elisa's arm. "She chased her singing career, leaving us behind over ten years ago."

"Wow, Sean, I am so sorry." Elisa felt like

she was the one who should comfort him. His expression was dark. He slid his sunglasses on. "It's good she keeps up with Blythe, right?"

"Keeps up with her?" Cynicism laced his tone. "Calling every few months, maybe only twice a year. Blythe's texts are more like a diary—a one-sided conversation. She doesn't know any different, so she takes what she can get when Mom does make time to respond."

"Huh, I understand that, surprisingly. My dad was the same way with my brother. Although, it was Dad who would take what he could get as far as time with Charlie went. My half brother resented my dad for remarrying, even though Charlie's mom was the one who wanted out of the marriage in the first place. It's tough for a kid to understand why a parent leaves." Elisa made a mental note to constantly remind the girls as they grew up that their parents had no choice in the matter of being absent. She glanced down at Ava, who was sleeping soundly.

Sean chuckled softly. "It's tough for an *adult* to understand why a parent disappears willingly."

"Someone choosing to go creates a massive hole—bigger than an old patio." Elisa should know. Her heart had felt hollowed out once she'd realized Chad had left her behind.

Hurt riddled Sean's face. She couldn't imagine

either of her parents walking away. They were the two people who'd given her a soft place to land.

This was not what Sean had expected to hash out today. And Elisa's attentive expression made him tense up. Pity was a thing of the past, and something he never wanted to receive. Especially since Blythe would undoubtedly feel the effect of pity—being treated as though she were made of glass, like he'd once felt. He had despised when his high school teachers gave him second and third chances, but not the other students, because his parents had fallen apart—literally and internally, it seemed. Folks in Rapid Falls had tried to help, but he'd felt all the weaker in the end. Now, he was being much too vulnerable with his employer. Silence passed between them, even with the construction going on out back.

"Please don't worry about Blythe. She is a rock star. Well-adjusted and loving life." Sean folded his arms across his chest.

"She's great." Elisa nodded in agreement. "My mom always tells me kids are resilient. I pray for strength for Lottie and Ava all the time. Your sister is a role model for them." She flashed a smile, but it wobbled with uncertainty.

"I am glad she doesn't resent Mom. Sometimes it feels like my own bitterness eats me alive." Sean's vulnerability slipped out. It had spread an ache in his heart, having been pent up so very long.

"I get that. I didn't know my brother and his wife, really. And I always held a bit of resentment for them because of the way Charlie treated my dad." She peered down at her thumb rubbing the handle. "But now, if I think about them too long—" Elisa's lashes fluttered, and she scanned the street, then the sky. "Regret is so heavy I can hardly breathe."

"Hurting for family—tough stuff." But Elisa's brother and sister-in-law were gone in the worst way.

Elisa smiled faintly. "My parents are in counseling. Sounds like it's going well for Dad. He's had a hard time." She inhaled deeply. "They're coming for Easter, so maybe you'll get to show off your work?" Her smile broadened, dissolving the gloom.

Sean exhaled relief. "Hoping to at least be close at that point."

"Good. And I am praying we get in some kind of rhythm by then, or else—" She pulled out her phone, paused as she read something, then stuck the phone in the stroller cup holder. "I might be commuting from Grangewood instead of Rapid Falls."

"What do you mean?"

"Plan B." She bobbed her eyebrows, then started moving down the walkway. "Move back home with my parents."

"Oh—" He let out a nervous chuckle. "I thought this was your home?" He gestured with a nod toward the covered porch.

"I am trying, believe me." She continued down the path, her ponytail swinging slightly. She grabbed her phone again and turned around. Machinery roared from the back. "Do you need the headphones back?"

"Nah." He strode toward the backyard again. "I'll borrow some." He wanted to say, *Enjoy Rapid Falls while you are still here*, but it only sounded passive-aggressive in his mind. It shouldn't. As long as he got this job in the books and was noticed by potential clients, Elisa Hartley's plan B was really none of his business.

Then why did his insides constrict when she spoke of potentially moving again? They had just talked about the consequences of people leaving a path of remorse behind. Maybe that was it. Elisa had turned the attention away from the heavy conversation only to leave a compression in his peace, like a deflated balloon holding on to its last bit of air.

Chapter Thirteen

Elisa caught most of the meeting and felt a sense of accomplishment by the time she turned the stroller down the sidewalk on Main Street. Ava was still soundly asleep. Every time Elisa checked on her, she'd inwardly giggle at the sight of the two-year-old with large noise-canceling headphones on. If only Elisa had brought her laptop, she could work at an outdoor table along Sweet Lula's storefront.

Ahead, the boutique door opened, and Sally appeared with an armful of baskets. Setting them on a wooden bookcase that sat under the shop's window, she pushed her billowy bangs from her face and spotted Elisa. "Hello, there. It's Elisa, right?"

Elisa nodded. When she noticed Ava sleeping, the woman put her finger to her lips and raised her manicured eyebrows. In a hushed voice, Sally remarked, "What a dumpling. I heard you have two sweet girls in your care."

"Yep. You don't have to whisper, though. Sean gave her those headphones. She's slept through a bunch of designers brainstorming." Elisa waved her phone.

"Sean is thoughtful, isn't he?" Her teeth glistened from a knowing grin, and Elisa assumed Sally, too, had a membership to the matchmaking knitting club. "Actually, he suggested I speak with you."

"Oh?" Elisa's heart leaped. A ridiculous reaction when she'd just spoken with Sean an hour ago.

"He thought you might be interested in updating my boutique." She held open the door, ushering Elisa inside with an eager gaze.

Forget the heart jump. A thread of frustration cut off any unexpected giddiness. Didn't she make herself clear to Sean, of all people, that she didn't need one more thing on her plate?

"You know, my firm acquires projects for me—"

"Sean mentioned that, but when it comes to opportunity, rules are just suggestions." She winked and gave a devious smile. At least it sounded like Sean may have been managing Sally's expectations. "This would be an excellent opportunity for you to make your mark in Rapid Falls."

Elisa opened her mouth to say she had no need to make a mark, and she really needed to leave, but then Sally began to elaborate on all her ideas for the space. While Elisa was internally scowling at first, she began to catch Sally's vision.

Sally spread her fingers across the uneven patch job she'd tried to cover up with dried wreaths. "So, what do you think?"

"Actually, I think this space has so much potential."

They began to discuss a budget, and Elisa pulled up some swatches on her phone. She ignored the niggling of her conscience, warning her to not offer up any more of her time. This quick conversation was all she would give. Even though transforming this shop into a cozy nook would be the next best thing to taking advantage of any remnant of quiet time she could scrounge up.

Something shifted inside Elisa. She warmed at the sight of Ava's tiny legs crossed at the ankles and the sound of Sally's boisterous cadence filling the space. She was smack-dab in the middle of others' lives, and while she'd once thought sharing the quiet with a man like Chad was all she ever wanted, being forced into this new rhythm seemed to have her confront all she'd thought about herself. Maybe she was allowed to go through the heartbreak not because she was meant to be alone, but to push her into a community unlike anything she'd ever wanted but perhaps like what she had needed. Because if there was one way Elisa could describe how she felt as she walked away from Sally's boutique, it was fullness in the sense of who she was, not in the busy schedule she was trying to maintain.

Sean spent the rest of the day trying to focus on the project. He couldn't help but replay the conversation with Elisa. Why did he share so much about his mom? Maybe he'd given away more than his headphones today; he'd given away a bit of the armor he'd reinforced over the years—the guard around his heart that fashioned him reliable and optimistic. He'd learned it from his father, a shield that warded off the reactive remarks of his mother before she had left, and after, what he could hear in her tone during their brief conversations.

Today, Sean took on some of the harder labor himself—pouring his energy into the physical work more than instructing and managing. By the afternoon, his neck and shoulders ached, and his collar was moist with sweat. The crew retreated to the work truck along the street for a break, so Sean headed to his truck for his lunch box. He'd worked clear past the lunch hour.

As he came around the front of the house, he noticed the stroller parked on the porch again. How long had Elisa been gone? Not that it mattered to him. But something she'd said had tucked away in the corner of his mind and clawed at his conscience. No matter how much he dug, raked or maneuvered the wheelbarrow today, Sean couldn't stop feeling a pang of guilt after Elisa had mentioned her change of heart over her late brother. Would Sean's own resentment for Mom come at the cost of some future regret?

Mom's selfish acts had dug a divide as wide and deep as the Pacific. The future was bleak as far as he could tell, and Sean's situation was far different than Elisa's.

He took out his sandwich, flung the empty lunch box in the truck bed and pulled down the tailgate.

"Hey, Sean!" Blythe walked up the drive, her hands clutching the straps of her backpack. "Are they back from preschool yet?"

"I have no idea." He began to unwrap his PB and J.

Elisa's SUV backed out of the garage. She rolled down her window. "Hey, Blythe. I am going to get Lottie now. We'll be back soon." She smiled at Sean. "I set the headphones on the patio table. It's complete chaos back there—in the very best way."

Sean gave a curt nod. "Absolutely. It's coming along nicely. We'll have a safe space for the girls to play soon."

"They'll be so excited." Elisa adjusted her

rearview mirror and said something to Ava. "See you all soon."

"Okay!" Blythe peered in the back window and waved to Ava. She turned around. "She's such a cutie."

"Sure is." Sean took a bite of his sandwich.

Blythe joined him on the tailgate. "I was thinking, what if I saved up my babysitting money for a ticket to Hawaii?"

"What?" Sean swallowed hard, almost choking on his bite. "Do you think you'll make enough for that?"

Blythe shrugged her shoulders. "I can get started. Even if it takes a year. Drawing those pictures of Hawaii made me think about how I'd love to visit."

"You wouldn't be able to go by yourself, Blythe," Sean said gently. And there was no way Sean could afford to go—both monetarily and emotionally. Landing on his mother's turf, the place she'd chosen over Rapid Falls, well, that would feel like approving Mom's choice. He pushed away the concern of what a year of declining health might hold for Mom.

Blythe cast a simmering gaze his way. As if trying to persuade him using her glare's intensity.

He shook his head and looked away. "You should see the backyard. Wouldn't recognize it."

Sean cringed. Changing the subject was not the most sensitive thing he could have done. Man, he had been way too vulnerable with Elisa earlier, and now he was dismissing his sister. "Blythe, I just don't want you to get hurt." She had no idea that Mom was not the success she imagined. Far from it. Her health problems would require any funds they might use for airfare. The news of her ill health had come as a surprise to Sean when his dad had shared it with him at the time his cancer took a turn for the worse.

Blythe swung her legs. "We don't have to go just for…her. You know, it's one of the top vacay destinations." She nudged him and smiled wide.

He laughed, thankful for her sense of humor. "Let me figure out this landscaping business first."

They chatted about some schoolwork while Sean finished eating. As they climbed down from the truck, Elisa's car appeared down the street.

"The Hartleys might not be here long-term," he blurted—not meaning to be so abrupt, but he just needed to get it out so Blythe would know.

"Oh, really?" Blythe crossed her arms over her torso and observed Elisa's car returning. "Are you sure? The girls' rooms are pretty unique to each of them. Lottie has a castle mural while Ava chose a jungle theme."

"Elisa said she'll move back with her parents if this doesn't go well. Just wanted you to know because it's easy to get attached—"

Blythe narrowed her eyes at him, and a knowing pause caused Sean's lungs to stop working. But all he could think about was the day she had to go to the hospital for a panic attack, and the following weeks of her depression. Nobody could be blamed except for her big brother and his poor judgment of character when it came to his girlfriend at the time.

Elisa pulled into the driveway, waving as she passed again.

"Don't worry about me, Sean." Blythe fetched her backpack out of the bed then closed the tailgate. "I have a feeling they are staying awhile. And no little kid can resist falling in love with me." She batted her eyelashes. "I am Rapid Falls's best babysitter. Worth staying for." She winked, giggled, then ran up the drive toward the garage.

Sean couldn't help but chuckle, shaking his head as he returned to the backyard. He hoped that Blythe was right. That the girls' happiness would be a good meter for Elisa to realize that Rapid Falls was a great place to raise her nieces. Sean pushed away the question poking at him— did he want them to stay only for his sister's sake?

Chapter Fourteen

That afternoon, Elisa was able to get work done while Blythe entertained the girls. She had tuned out the backyard noise, for the most part, as she worked on concepts for her new client. A steady thumping drew her away from her computer screen. She peered through the blinds and down to what was once a patio, now a raked patch of soil. Toward the side of the house, Sean was setting up orange construction fence in a path from the gate to a leveled area on the upper terrace of the yard. There were flags staked around the first support posts of the playset. A large pile of cedar mulch sat nearby.

She watched Sean carefully mark off the safe path for the girls to reach their playset during the rest of the build. After speaking with him about his mom earlier, Elisa had grown homesick for her parents all the more. Even when her wedding fell apart, Mom and Dad had put their lives on hold to help her through the devastating reality that she had been left behind.

Sean had been old enough to feel the immediate repercussions of being abandoned by his mother. Some teens may have spiraled into rebellion at that kind of loss. But instead, Sean had turned out to be a responsible, loving caregiver to his sister.

Elisa pulled herself away from spying on the handsome landscape architect in her backyard and headed downstairs. There was no obvious movement outdoors that matched the continuous thumping. It was coming from inside the house.

Music filled the living room. The girls were dressed in princess dresses while Blythe shone a flashlight on each girl as they jumped and twirled and…jumped. Ah, the thumping noise.

"Auntie!" Lottie flared out her long dress with handfuls of the material in each hand, then twirled, while Ava thumped, thumped, thumped along the hardwood floor. "We are dancing!"

Blythe grinned and held up the flashlight. "Works as a spotlight for the little stars."

"Ah, I see."

"Watch, watch!" Ava pushed loose curls from around her temples with both tiny hands and widened her arms. She started singing a song from their favorite princess movie, but most of her words were jumbled. Lottie belted out the lyrics. They held hands and spun in a circle while they sang—hardly in harmony, but nonetheless, absolutely adorably.

"I haven't seen them so enthusiastic—ever." Amused, Elisa sank down on the couch next to Blythe. "You have a way with them."

"I am the best babysitter ever. Just wait 'til Lottie's in elementary school. I am great with homework, too." Her pink lips formed a sly smile.

"Oh, well, that's quite a ways away." Actually, it wasn't. Next fall, Lottie would be in kindergarten. Elisa's stomach rolled at the flash-forward to being a full-fledged guardian of school-age children. "I will definitely need all the help I can get then."

"Good." Blythe's cheeks grew rosy, her braces glistened and her freckles bounced as she scrunched her nose in an affectionate way. "I just love Lottie and Ava. They are the best little girls."

"They are."

Although they were talking about the girls, Elisa couldn't take her eyes off the teen sitting next to her. Blythe exuded confidence, speaking as though this was a permanent arrangement. Elisa shifted in her seat, ignoring the possibility of plan B and its effect on a girl she was getting to know well.

Her nieces collapsed on the area rug and panted.

"We're thirsty," Lottie groaned.

Blythe switched off the flashlight but gasped and held up her finger. "Yikes, my nail." Her thumbnail was jagged, a sliver hanging off. "That's a stubborn flashlight switch."

Elisa rose and walked to the kitchen saying, "I'll get the girls some water and a nail file for you." After filling up Ava's sippy and a small cup for Lottie, she rummaged through her purse and pulled out her cosmetic bag. "I can't stand snaggy nails, so I keep files on hand for such an instance." The girls and Blythe sat around the kitchen table. Elisa handed Blythe an unused disposable emery board, then brought drinks to the girls.

Blythe was a bit awkward with the file. Just running it back and forth.

"If you tilt it, like this—" Elisa showed her how to shape her nail by holding the file at an angle on the underside of the nail "—you'll round it out and then it won't get caught on things."

Blythe giggled. "I wondered how people got their nails to look like that." She furrowed her brow. "To be honest, I usually just bite mine."

Elisa almost shared how her mom had taught her to care for her nails in sixth grade, but bit her tongue. Blythe didn't have a mom to help her with that.

"I wanna try," Lottie exclaimed.

Elisa grabbed another unused file and said, "Here, Lottie. Let me see those nails." Elisa began to file the tiny fingernails, and Blythe continued to file her own.

"I want nail polish, too." Lottie watched intently. Ava sucked her sippy but splayed her hand on the table to be next.

"I don't have any fun nail polish, girls. I'm sorry." She only had clear, strengthening polish.

"I have some fun colors at home," Blythe said. "Maybe we can have a mani-pedi day. Elisa, you can teach all of us about beauty care."

Elisa laughed at that. "Oh, I am not much of a pamperer."

"But you are a woman. You know more than us." Blythe crawled her fingers across the table and teasingly pinched Ava's cheek. They laughed. Elisa joined them, too, but a lump lodged in her throat. Blythe was this lively young girl barreling forward with all the joy she could muster, regardless of the hardship of the past. And really, the hardship of the present, too. Because what teen girl would be A-OK without a mom to help her navigate growing into a woman?

Elisa may have been the adult sitting around the table that afternoon, but she hardly felt like she was in a place to teach at this moment. Sure, she might know nail care and beauty tips, but she was learning so much from Blythe. And her brother, really. They'd overcome both of their parents' leaving, and instead of shrinking away from others, Blythe and Sean were happy to be connected to the community and the newbie residents. In fact, Elisa felt most welcomed to Rapid Falls by the Peterses. Something about Blythe anchoring herself in the Hartleys' upcoming future made Elisa curious if friendship with the two siblings might make this new family life easier.

If she stayed.

Sean worked on the playset until dusk, then began to pack up his tools, knowing that Blythe had already left to walk home about an hour ago. He wanted to get as much done as he could to be sure the playset was ready for next week.

The light on the garage flipped on, casting the gate's long shadow across the back lawn. The wrought iron hinges squealed as the shadow shifted, and Elisa appeared. She wore a fleece jacket, and her hair was piled high in her typical messy bun.

"Hey, there. You're working hard into the night." She glanced upward at the indigo sky streaked with orange clouds above a blistering horizon. "Or at least, into the sunset. Wow, such beautiful skies."

"Just wait until nighttime. Stargazing is a favorite pastime at the Peters house. Blythe, Dad and I would make popcorn and lie out on a blanket just to count shooting stars. Better than the movies." He stuffed his hands in his pockets, chiding himself for continually opening up to this woman. "I am sure you have great skies in Grangewood."

"Yep, we do. It's the perk of living farther from the city. But in the summer, I am usually ready for bed by the time it's dark."

"Speaking of summer nights, I thought it might be nice to incorporate a traditional woodburning firepit in the back near the evergreens. Roasting marshmallows on a wood fire is the best. Figured the girls would love it."

"Sounds good." She walked around the almost completed playset. "This is going to be great. I appreciate you considering the girls in all of this."

"Of course." He spread out a clump of mulch with his boot, then joined Elisa on the edge of the space. "So, how did Blythe do today?"

"Amazing, as usual." Elisa's smile was dazzling—more than a sky filled with stars. Sean had to admit that the woman who'd made her old house beautiful was no less a beauty herself. "Blythe is insisting on a mani-pedi party. I was going to see if you wouldn't mind if she stayed late one night next week?"

"Oh, yeah, that's fine. Maybe you and I could go shopping in Waterloo for the firepit stones. Would be great to have your input."

"Well, Blythe thinks I am the expert on beauty care and wanted me to help." Elisa didn't appear completely comfortable with the words that came out of her mouth. And Sean wasn't comfortable with them, either. He had warned Blythe not to get attached. Was she mature enough to foresee the consequences if Elisa ended up leaving?

Sean drew near and inhaled deeply. Cedar mixed with Elisa's floral perfume. He was kinda bummed that the cedar was ever-present. "Blythe's a big dreamer. Always figuring out how to get the most out of life. Don't feel like you have to follow along if she tries to rope you in."

Elisa shook her head and held her hand up in the most serious way. "Oh, no, not at all. I didn't mean to sound like I didn't want to help her. I—I am honored, really. She is such a great kid. And I am happy to give her any advice you might not be able to."

"Oh, really?" He cocked his eyebrow, slightly annoyed but also intrigued by this side of Elisa—not reserved or resistant, but forthcoming and generous. "I'll admit, I don't have a clue at helping her achieve the messy bun look." He reached out and tapped her hair.

She laughed and feigned an offended look—

her mouth dropped open, but her eyes were filled with amusement. "They don't teach you that in the landscaping biz? It was my first lesson during late-night studying hours in college." She batted her eyelashes and fanned her fingers out on either side of her face. "I think I've aced it, so I am more than willing to help your sister."

He chuckled, dropped his gaze from Elisa's cute display of humor and kicked his toe on the ground. When he looked up at her again, her smile had faded, and she nibbled on her lip. Insecurity flashed in her eyes.

"I appreciate your willingness to help, Elisa, really, I do. But I just don't want her to get too attached—"

"Oh, I don't want to intrude. She's that age where girls could use a good mentor—" She swallowed hard. "She seemed pretty eager for my advice. I don't mind at all."

"But I don't want you to feel obligated."

"Of course."

"And I don't want her to get her hopes up."

"Hopes up?"

Embarrassment flamed in Sean's face as he realized the distinction between Kylie and Elisa. Kylie had almost been his fiancée; Elisa was his employer. "That…that you are going to be here for the long term. You mentioned commuting from your parents' instead."

Her brow broke into several lines as she seemed to search for words. "Like I said before, I can't even think about next week." A cynicism crossed her features. "But being prepared for plan B is always a good thing." She glanced up at the fading light in the sky. "I've literally been left in the dark before. No fun. Now I always have a proverbial flashlight tucked in my back pocket. You know, always prepared for whatever life throws at me."

"Resourceful," Sean summed it up. He wondered if she was talking about losing her brother or the day Chad didn't show up. Suddenly, Sean felt like the impostor. This wasn't his yard, or his business.

Elisa stepped closer and laid a hand on his arm. "Seriously, Sean. If you don't want me to help Blythe, I understand. But as a woman who was once her age, I know that type of advice is so helpful. Helps a girl feel confident in who she is both inside and out."

She was genuine and spoke from experience and truth. If there was one thing he'd learned about Elisa Hartley, it was that no matter what life threw at her, she brimmed with a quiet confidence. Admitting that she'd equipped herself with an escape plan was the same kind of thing he'd been doing all his adult life. But instead of escaping, Sean had built a fortress around his heart and extended it to Blythe also. Standing in the comforting presence of Elisa Hartley was testing the importance of that wall right now.

Elisa slid her hand down his arm. "Just let me know, okay?" The flush in her cheeks rivaled the crimson in the sky. Did she feel the same intensity that coursed through his veins?

That kind of rush threatened to destroy his fortress in one fell swoop. Then he'd be exposed to another future rejection, another person walking farther and farther away, and an innocent sister who might just break at the devastation of losing yet another female role model in her life.

"Okay, good night, Elisa." Sean puffed out his chest and turned away before releasing all his breath. It was getting dark. He'd better get home to Blythe—Sean's only sure and steadfast plan in his immediate future.

Chapter Fifteen

After attending services at St. George's on Sunday, Elisa and the girls walked to the park. She had spoken with a few of the preschool board members, and now she had to control the many ideas forming in her mind for the old annex. Her brain was full enough.

On the way home, they took some long overdue thank-you notes to Marge. Their bubbly neighbor was excited to see them and insisted they come inside. Her breakfast nook had all sorts of toys that appeared to be older than Elisa. Marge explained that she had held on to her own kids' toys for future generations to enjoy.

"Now, you girls feel free to play with whatever you like. My Jane said you two are very creative." Marge winked at Elisa, her dimple deepening with her delightful smile.

"Oh, we don't need to stay—" Elisa should

have mailed the notes instead. She wasn't expecting a social engagement.

"How about a cup of tea while the girls play?" She didn't wait for an answer and began filling up the kettle.

Elisa lowered herself to the stool at the counter and watched the girls inspect the bins as if they'd never seen rag dolls and wooden blocks before.

Marge tapped her nails on her tiled counter across from Elisa. "I can't believe how different your backyard looks." Her blue eyes twinkled. "That Sean Peters is something else, huh?"

Elisa couldn't help but grin at her unsubtle prodding. "He's doing a great job."

Marge pulled out some cups and tea bags. "Now, I don't like to brag, but I've been practicing a new muffin recipe for the orchard, and I think it turned out delicious."

"Orchard?"

"Hudson Orchard. It's just outside of town. I am the manager at the orchard café, but not until the fall. However, the Hudsons are hosting our community Easter egg hunt this year. The muffins are for that. I kind of overdid it." She pushed two large tins along the counter. "I insist you take some with you."

"That's a lot of muffins."

"But you have all those young men working in your yard. And Blythe has a sweet tooth. Inherited it from her mother." Marge's brightness dimmed a bit. "But I would never tell her that. Poor dear." Marge cleared her throat and leaned in, positioning her head away from the girls. "To think Blythe had to stay overnight in the hospital because of the grief she's gone through?" Marge shook her head and sighed.

Elisa didn't want to gossip about the Peterses. Her heart lurched at the thought of Blythe going to the hospital. Something must have happened more recently than their mother's initial leaving, since she was only two at that time. "Blythe's been such a light around our house. And very optimistic about helping her mom's career with her drawing skills. I hope she's okay now."

"Seems to be. Took a long time to get over Kylie leaving." Marge pursed her lips. "That woman was practically a sister to Blythe."

Elisa recalled Blythe talking about Sean's ex-girlfriend and the girl's obvious disappointment that Kylie hadn't stuck around.

"Kylie stole the heart of many around here. Seemed a future resident...and bride." She raised her eyebrows. "But the woman decided Rapid Falls wasn't for her. Supposedly working abroad now. Blythe was too young to understand when her own mother left, but when Kylie broke things off with Sean, I am not sure who took it worse—Sean or his sister. Sean blamed himself for Blythe's panic attacks." The kettle whistled. Marge busied with getting the tea ready.

Elisa slid off the stool and checked on the girls. They were playing with old ponies and a stable that was hand-painted, not decorated with stick-on decals. She glanced out the side of the bay window facing her backyard.

"I have appreciated Sean's work on my house—" she turned to Marge "—and his help with my girls. I've gotten to know him. He's one of the most compassionate people I've met in a long time." She turned back to the view of the neatly posted construction fence for the girls' safety. "I can imagine how much he hurt seeing Blythe struggling."

"It was a tough time. Blythe stayed here after school until someone was home the rest of that school year." She sighed as she poured the steaming water. "And then Howard's cancer the following year—" She wagged her head. "Too much for kids to take on, but Sean and Blythe amaze me every day." Her blue eyes swam against the rise of her cheeks from a gentle smile.

Elisa pulled out her stool. She admitted, "I don't know what I'd do without them."

"I do worry about Sean, though. Weighed down with worry for his sister. And blame." Marge set a pretty teacup down in front of Elisa. "Here you go, dear."

"Thank you." Elisa half expected Marge to knit the conversation with a matchmaking remark. Yet a melancholic silence hung between them. Marge's concern for Sean seeped into Elisa's heart, and she prayed for his peace. Sean had no idea that Elisa had suffered similar heartbreak. She wondered if sharing her story with him would bring him any comfort. After all, he had done the same for her with parenting advice.

Elisa sipped her tea and savored the bergamot warmth. Being understood was a powerful step in healing. She thanked God for showing her that today. And she thanked Him for Marge's insistence on inviting them inside for a while.

The next morning, Elisa and the girls ate the most delicious cranberry orange muffins Elisa had ever tasted. Obviously, Marge was an excellent baker. The doorbell rang while Elisa cleaned up. Lottie and Ava ran to the door and bounced on their toes as they waited for Elisa to answer it.

She could see Blythe's figure through the mottled glass. "It's Blythe. I can see her strawberry blond hair." Elisa opened the door, and the teenager was attacked by two little girls giving her bear hugs around her thighs.

"Good morning," Blythe exclaimed. "We are going to have the best spring break ever."

The girls cheered, and they all entered the living room.

Before Elisa closed the door, Sean appeared down the walkway, carrying his toolbox in one hand and a to-go mug in the other. He held up his cup with a nod. "Good morning, Elisa."

She stepped outside. "It's a beautiful day. Can't believe it's going to get up to seventy today."

"Perfect spring weather." He took a sip of his drink. "Are you officing here today? We are going to finish up the playset first thing. Thought we could do the big reveal for the girls after lunch." He sounded all business.

Last time they had spoken, Elisa found herself waffling between being a possible mentor to his sister and being the woman who'd made it pretty clear she wasn't tied to this town. After yesterday with Marge, Elisa had a sinking feeling that she was the antagonist in Sean's eyes.

Music spilled from the ajar front door.

"Sounds like the pre-festivities are beginning." Sean craned his neck and peeked inside the front window. "Yep, they are having fun regardless of a swing set and a slide."

"Ah, don't worry, your playset will be so much more fun."

"For the resident interior designer, I am sure?" He bounced his eyebrows. "Send all distractions outside."

"You've got that right." A laugh was bubbling in her throat, but the fluttering in her stomach had her tense up and swallow whatever reaction Sean Peters induced. He was handsome as ever. She almost forgot that she was not on spring break like the girls. Sitting in the warm sunshine, discussing a reveal that could rival Christmas morning to two little girls, and admiring the jovial Mr. Peters had tripped up Elisa's usual business-as-usual stance.

She turned to go inside. "Oh, wait, I have some muffins from Marge for your crew. Want to just come through the house?"

"Nah, I have my boots on. I'll grab them later." Sean continued toward the side yard. The overactive flutters in Elisa's stomach finally settled. "Marge's muffins are good incentive to work hard."

Elisa did laugh at that—a ridiculously high-pitched, melodic laugh that sounded less like Elisa Hartley and more like a school friend of Blythe's. Silly and girlish. But the dimple appearing in Sean's stubbly cheek as his lips turned up in amusement was the perfect boyish reaction to her giddiness. Once she went inside and closed the door, she refrained from leaning on it to ground herself to reality like some old movie heroine. Neither Sean nor Elisa needed any distractions in their lives right now. Focusing on the girls—all three of them—was the most important thing.

* * *

Sean ran his hand over the surface of the flagstone heaped between Elisa's house and Marge's. Marge waved from her back porch as she watered some fresh pots. Sean skirted around the stone and crossed over to her.

"Hey, there, Sean. Looks like you've made a mess of Elisa's yard, through and through."

"It's a beautiful mess, don't you think?" Sean leaned on the back of an old wicker love seat.

"Your father would think so." She set her watering can down and rubbed her hands together. "He'd be so proud of you. As long as you don't put up a fence." Her syrupy laugh warmed him, as always.

"Never."

"Good. I might insist on a bench so I can watch the girls play on that fantastic playset. They are sweet as can be. And with my grandchildren growing as fast as weeds, it's nice seeing younger kids around." Marge's eyes glistened. She and Lula had taken turns watching Blythe and Sean as they grew up. Marge was the closest person Sean had to a grandmother. And the one person who knew his mom the best.

"I am not sure Elisa's committed to staying here that long, Marge." Déjà vu was pressing down on him, but at least this time he had a heads-up from Elisa. Kylie hadn't been as gracious. He clenched his jaw, chiding himself. "It's a shame, because Blythe is enjoying the girls so much." And Elisa, it seemed. A bitter root, too familiar, strangled any thought of affection.

"Blythe shines bright, Sean. She can handle more now than ever." Marge sat down and folded her hands in her lap. "That's what I write in my letters to Cheri."

Sean bristled at the mention of his mother's name. "You still write her?" He stepped around the love seat and sat, leaning his elbows on his knees. Marge nodded with a sympathetic smile. "Does she write back?"

"Oh, once in a blue moon." She squinted and looked away. "I am concerned by her handwriting lately. It's hardly legible." She cast a watchful look at Sean, only out of courtesy. Marge knew she'd plunged into turbulent waters by the comment. "And the letter was filled with remorse, I tell you."

"Enough, Marge." He gripped his legs with tight fists.

"I am not saying I don't agree with your hurt, dear, but I do think you should consider some forgiveness. It will do both you and Blythe a world of good."

"Forgive Mom?" He raised his eyebrows at this woman whom he'd just come visited for a friendly chat, not a lecture.

"Elisa was telling me about Blythe's dream to help your mom's singing career."

"Why were you talking about that?"

"We were just getting more acquainted, that's all. She's impressed with Blythe. And when she mentioned Blythe's hope, I just couldn't help but think it's time for a reality check around here." She leaned her elbow on the arm of the chair and pressed forward, staring with wise, sharp eyes. "Blythe's fantasy world is a product of secrets, Sean. You've got to get real with her. With yourself. Healing's been long overdue."

"We are doing just fine, Marge." Sean rose to leave. He didn't need this right now. They were doing the best they could. "Like Elisa said, Blythe is impressive. And that has nothing to do with the mother she never had."

"Your mom wrote that you aren't returning her calls."

"It's been maybe one…in six months."

"Well, she said she doesn't blame you. But I couldn't help but wonder—" Marge pushed herself to standing and locked eyes with him. "What might healing look like for all of you?"

"I need to get to work."

"Elisa said something else, Sean. She admitted you have been the most compassionate guy to the girls—to her." Marge neared him and pressed a hand on his arm, the same fingers that had once held his hand as he crossed the street to head home after she babysat. "You've almost got what it takes, Sean Peters—'And be ye kind one to another, tenderhearted, *forgiving one another*, even as God for Christ's sake hath forgiven you.'" A benevolent smile grew on her face, but her eyes only intensified with wisdom.

Chapter Sixteen

Elisa managed to work for a solid hour before the banging began. But this time she was excited for the noise because it meant the crew was finishing up the playset, and soon, all the thumping from downstairs would transfer to the mulched play area outside.

Elisa peeked through the slats of the window blind. The backyard was in utter chaos. Materials everywhere. The patio was now leveled dirt, and a skid loader was poised next to piles of gravel, mulch and decomposed granite. Stress crept in as thoughts of her own unfinished projects bombarded her mind. She faced her computer screen. A social media notification popped up—a message containing a picture from her college friend Betsy.

I can't believe this.

Elisa leaned forward, and as she focused, her insides melded to her stomach like iron to a lead weight.

Chad sat under a cabana roof in sunny Florida. The girl he'd met in the Caribbean was holding out her ring finger with a big fat diamond shining in the forefront of the picture.

The last time Elisa had spoken with Chad, he'd used the excuse that he hadn't wanted to commit, and when he missed his flight, he'd taken it as a sign that he shouldn't get married. Sure, he had met this woman at that point, but he insisted that she was only another sign that he wasn't invested in the quiet dream of a Victorian remodel and small-town living. But was it really all about the plan they'd had? Or was it more about Elisa, the introverted designer who was just fine reading books side by side instead of heading out on the town in the evening?

The truth was, Chad hadn't been invested in *Elisa*. It wasn't about commitment or marriage. It was about Elisa.

Tears stung the backs of her eyes. Every single thud from outside rattled her last nerve. Elisa had retreated to Rapid Falls for a fresh start— and she had hoped for some peace and quiet, too. But now she was sitting here, in a room that was once meant to be the master suite of happy newlyweds, working away as a commuting mother-wannabe, while the guy she'd built her dream around was off proposing to a woman he barely knew. All the Band-Aids of her broken heart were ripped off to expose that she hadn't really changed at all. She was still the rejected one. Caring for the girls was the only difference.

Sean shouted across the yard, and the skid loader's engine roared through the walls. Work, that was all she could do—should do. Elisa tried to focus, but her temples throbbed, and a stabbing pain radiated from behind her eyes.

A loud crash made her jump in her chair.

That was it.

Elisa didn't need these disruptions right now. She could hardly think straight. Storming down the stairs, she plastered a two-second smile when all three of the girls looked over at her from the toy corner in the living room, then marched through the four-season room to go out back. But the patio was gone. Elisa groaned. She was surrounded, in her own house. Changing course, she went through the kitchen, out the garage and down the path lined with orange construction fence leading to the playset. Sean was hanging up a swing.

"Sean," Elisa said, but the noise of the skid loader drowned out her voice. "Sean!" She yelled just as the skid loader shut off. Everyone turned and stared at her.

"Elisa, what's going on?" Sean crossed over to her.

She gave a weak grin to the construction workers, then stared into Sean's questioning eyes. "Is there any way you all can just call it quits for the day? Maybe the week? I… I need time to process—" She pressed her fingers on either side of her head.

"Process? What?"

"Do you realize how much work I have to do?" She looked at him with one eye, the other one squeezed shut as she tried to prevent the pain from taking over her face.

"Hey, we are trying to help with that." Sean's comforting smile almost shone away the gloom filling Elisa's heart right now. "Your boss is going to be amazed with the gem of the tour."

Elisa couldn't force a smile if she tried. "Okay, Sean." Her words came out condescending. "Sorry, my head is just pounding."

Sean cradled her elbow, and offered, "Let me get you some pain meds. We could go for a walk while they finish up with the machinery? We could consider it a business meeting… I have an idea I wanted to share with you."

"It's going to take a few blocks to get away from the noise." She tapped her head.

"How about we drive instead? I can treat you to a latte and a table for two in the sunshine?" he suggested. "I need to do some work along Main Street, anyway. You can have some alone time while I water the petunias."

"I am not going to be much of a conversationalist. But that sounds kind of nice."

They grabbed some pain medicine from Sean's toolbox, a bottle of water from an ice chest, and headed out the side gate. Elisa grabbed her purse from the kitchen counter quietly, so as to not disturb the girls, and met Sean at his truck.

She had wanted everyone to leave so she could be alone to sort out her disappointment. But even for an introvert, the idea of being alone with thoughts of Chad and his new fiancée didn't seem like the best way to handle the situation.

A coffee break with quiet company seemed a better alternative.

Sean drove, admiring the many spring blooms spilling from the front porches. He took care driving with all the kids on bikes zipping by. Elisa kept her face glued to the passenger window. He couldn't tell if her eyes were open or closed. He pulled in a space on Main, parked, then hopped out to open Elisa's door.

"How's the headache?"

"Still here." She tapped her temples and the crease between her eyebrows.

"Why don't you grab that table under the awning, and I'll get our coffees?"

She nodded, took his hand and stepped down. He led her to a table, her hand still in his grasp. Elisa appeared distraught and fatigued; he couldn't help but hold on a little longer than usual.

"Thanks, Sean." She smiled weakly, squeezed his hand, then pulled her sunglasses out from her purse.

Sean jogged inside and ordered. By the time he brought the lattes out, color had returned to Elisa's face, but the distressed dip of her mouth hadn't disappeared. "Here you go." He set the cup on the wrought iron table. He noticed Sally crossing the street as if he'd just missed her. "Did she bombard you with ideas for the boutique?"

"Bombard? No, I like talking shop with her. She's got an amazing eye." Elisa sipped the drink and sat back, lifting her long blond hair up and over the back of the chair. "If my boss didn't keep me so busy…" She glanced up and down Main Street. "There are some opportunities in Rapid Falls that intrigue me."

"Like?"

"St. George's annex, the boutique, a chance to help with the new custom builds on the south side of town. Oh, hey—" She lifted her sunglasses onto her head. A robust smile brightened her face. "You could get some business, too. Landscape is always the next step for a new homeowner. Have you thought about promoting business there?"

Sean shrugged his shoulders, trying to focus on her words and not…her. "They are just breaking ground. I have a couple calls in to see about being contracted for the jobs."

"Good." Elisa lifted the coffee to her lips and faintly smiled. "Sweet Lula's is exactly what I needed. I felt like the walls were going to cave in on me."

"This is where Blythe and I retreat also." He ran his fingers around the lid of his to-go cup. "Sometimes to get rid of headaches—" he gave a lopsided smile "—and other times, to see people who know us. Who knew Dad. I guess Lula and Marge, really. They're like family. Blythe jokes and calls them her grannies."

"That's sweet. Marge really cares for her, too." Elisa's teeth rested on her lip, and she fiddled with her cup. "I had a good conversation with Marge yesterday."

Sean recalled what Marge had said. They'd talked about Blythe. And his mom. "Can't wait to finish up the project so she can rest assured there will be no fence."

Elisa's laugh assured him that ignoring the unspoken subjects of her conversation yesterday was a good move.

She raised a brow and sipped her latte again. "Honestly, I can't wait until the tour is over. Never in a million years did I think this dream project would be literal stomping grounds for rambunctious little girls."

Sean grimaced, recalling her plan B. "Did the stress of the tour bring on the migraine today? I mean, besides the noise from outside."

Elisa pressed her cheek to her shoulder and drew a circle with her finger on the table. "Oh, the migraine has been in the works since November."

"For what it's worth, you've done so much with the place already. It won't take long to tidy it up for the tour. And Blythe can always take the girls to our house—" He bit his tongue as he tried to hold back his next question. *If you leave, will it be before or after the tour?* Heat traveled up his neck at the tiny voice in his head wanting to convince her to stay as long as possible. For Blythe's sake, of course.

Elisa squinted into the sunny streetscape. "Blythe is such a help with the girls. To think I would have never gotten to know her if—" She paused, sipped her drink and sighed. "I would have sold the place a long time ago if it weren't for the girls."

Sean had more than a suspicion that the migraine-in-the-works from November—a specific date in November, in fact—had nothing to do with the house, but everything to do with Chad.

Maybe Sean should tell her he drove her away from the church that day. This would be awkward, but didn't she need to know he was fully aware of the subtext in their conversations?

"Elisa, look, there's something I want to tell you—"

She inhaled deeply, set her elbows on the table between them and looked at him straight on. "Yes. Please tell me about this idea you have. Your enthusiasm back at the house rivaled Lottie's and Ava's excitement when Blythe came to the door this morning."

Sean set his cup down and folded his hands on the table. Whatever distress clouded Elisa's countenance earlier was gone. She was genuinely interested in moving this conversation along into business talk. Sean would not be the one to add to the migraine she'd finally conquered. Why bring up a wedding that had never happened?

Chapter Seventeen

Elisa finally felt better and didn't want to think about anything but the creamy coffee in her hands and Sean's considerate offer to take her away to this peaceful day on Main Street. She could hardly remember why she'd gotten upset this morning. Or at least, she wasn't going to think on anything that waited for her back on her computer right now.

She had little motivation to get back to work. Her clients were high-maintenance and her boss, even worse. If there was any work Elisa wanted to do at all, it was to meet with Sally and finalize some details for her boutique remodel. When they'd talked earlier, Elisa had agreed to a couple of early morning meetings with Sally this week. Maybe nothing would come from it, but Elisa was more intrigued by the small-town shop than any project she'd been involved with in months—besides her own house, of course.

This was where God had placed her—in an idyllic streetscape with this attractive man and good conversation to keep her from fixating on the dream that never was. And unlike Chad the accountant, Sean the landscape architect could talk design with her. Exactly her cup of tea, or latte. Sean may only be a hired consultant, but today, he was a handsome distraction from Elisa's sore spot in her heart.

"So, tell me your idea before we need to go." Her cell phone vibrated with a meeting reminder in one hour.

Sean's hazel eyes flashed with excitement. "Okay, you won't believe what I found while I was at the salvage yard in Waterloo. Check this out." He took out his phone and showed her a picture of a large wrought iron garden structure like a gazebo. "This dates to the same time as your house, I believe."

"Sean, that really won't go with the cutting-edge design we talked about."

"I know. But wait." He opened another file with a pergola containing some of the wrought iron elements from the historic structure. "Wouldn't a unique pergola tie everything together? It could sit at the very center of the yard, kind of the focal point from all angles."

Chad had wanted a pergola.

All the emotions Elisa had tamped down with

a solid dose of distraction suddenly erupted at the mention of that pesky dream element of Chad's. Tears flooded her eyes and a small sob hitched in the back of her throat. Sean had been elaborating on the pergola and stopped midsentence, seemingly well aware of Elisa's emotion. The residual ache from her migraine finally released all the tears she'd held back.

"Hey, there." Sean set his phone down and grabbed her hand. "What's the matter, Elisa?"

She wiped her cheek with the back of her hand. "Pergola. He wanted one. I had spent hours shopping sites and catalogs for the perfect one." Her words were choppy, forced out on small hiccups of crying.

Sean scooted closer and squeezed her hand. "I am sorry."

"I bought the house for us. For our new life once we got married. But he realized he didn't want the commitment when he missed his flight before our wedding. He said it was a sign that he wasn't supposed to get married. Didn't show up on our wedding day at all. But now…now he's—" She lowered her face as her sobs became too strong to swallow.

"You don't have to say anything," Sean gently spoke. He rubbed her back as she cried into her palm.

"He's engaged. To the person he left me for."

She sniffled and then wiped both of her eyes with her hands. "It wasn't about commitment. It was about me."

The only people who had seen Elisa Hartley cry so hard, besides Sean, were her parents and the driver of that old Mustang.

Fear gripped her, and she stared hard at the table. Looking up at Sean trying to console her with a back rub and a tender voice seemed an even more cowardly act than bursting into tears before him. Elisa had no desire to be known this way—as a whimpering, heartbroken woman who depended so much on the care of others. She didn't want to be so foolish as to look to someone else for her contentedness. There was a reason she liked being alone—it was safer than trusting another person to fulfill a need.

Without waiting for her to look up, Sean tucked his finger under her chin and tilted her face. He said quietly, "I am so sorry, Elisa. It hurts when someone we love turns our plans upside down." She searched his eyes, recognizing pure empathy in his words, his gaze.

And the thing was, she knew he understood.

Sean didn't want to grow close to this woman. But the same protective reaction he had for Blythe rose in him for Elisa now. Anger coursed through his veins at the thought of Chad being so insensitive. After the sorrowful drive across Grangewood that day, Chad had become the biggest loser in Sean's book. And that was before Sean even knew Elisa.

Now this amazing woman impressed Sean with her talented eye for design and her loving care for her nieces. If only Sean could trust his judgment when it came to matters of the heart.

"I know what it's like to trust someone, only to realize the relationship was lopsided." He winced at his admission. Memories of his broken relationship causing Blythe so much pain twisted his gut.

Elisa calmed her breathing and took another sip of her coffee. "It always hurt so badly to watch the pain my brother caused my dad. And even though it's different, I sometimes think I have an idea of what it feels like—to love someone who refuses to love you back."

A cynical chuckle escaped Sean's lips. "Believe me, I know. And the toughest thing was the effect it had on my whole family. My ex Kylie, whom I met in college, got really close to Blythe. Kylie worked in Rapid Falls one summer. She had lived above Sally's boutique and helped manage the business while Sally vacationed. We were...pretty serious. And Blythe finally had a consistent female figure in her life. Kylie was so good with Blythe." He shook his head at the memory of Blythe packing up for sleepovers at Kylie's. "Blythe even started calling her 'sister.' We had talked about getting engaged, and I was waiting for the right moment to pop the question. But—" He clenched his teeth, daring to look at Elisa.

She just nodded for him to continue. And everything within him said it was good for her to hear this. Not only because he really did know how she felt, but so she would understand how important it was to maintain Blythe's expectations. "Kylie said she was suffocated by our small-town plan. She didn't want to live in Rapid Falls forever, and she just couldn't see herself being content in the long run." He breathed in deeply, stuttering on the remnants of hurt at her rejection. "I was committed to stay here with Blythe and Dad. There was no other option. So, we broke up. And Blythe was completely devastated. It was as if she had lost the mother she never knew, as if Kylie walking out was a reenactment of our mom leaving her."

Elisa shook her head. "Poor Blythe. Marge had said something about the hospital. She's been through quite a bit, it sounds like."

"The summer Kylie left was right before fifth grade for Blythe. She'd been going through a lot of adolescent changes, but also having a tough time at school with some other kids. Kylie had been her rock. And when she removed herself from our lives, Blythe's panic attacks began. One day, she couldn't breathe. Dad was so scared. He called me from the emergency room. I will never forget how hopeless I felt." He removed his glasses and rubbed the bridge of his nose. "Not worth it. Bringing someone into Blythe's life like that—when she'd lived her whole life with a void caused by our mother—well, there's no reason she needs to endure the pain of yet another woman disappearing." He put his glasses on and focused on Elisa.

She narrowed her eyes as color crept across her cheeks. Elisa didn't have to read between the lines. Sean had clearly spilled what he had been worried about this whole time.

"I… I don't want to do anything to hurt Blythe."

He barely nodded. The implication he made—that Elisa might be considered Kylie's replacement—grew an awkwardness between them.

Elisa's phone trilled. She glanced at the screen and stood. "Look, I can't promise anything. But the last thing I want to do is hurt someone like we've been hurt." She reached out and held his hand. "Especially Blythe. Don't worry, Sean. I'll take care. And if we leave—" her brow tipped up in hesitation "—Blythe will not feel abandoned. Promise." She answered the phone and began to walk toward the truck. "Hi, Mom, how's it going?"

All Sean could do was pray. Pray that Elisa knew what she was talking about. Because as much as he would have liked to believe that Elisa Hartley would cause minimal destruction if she moved away from Rapid Falls, his heart knew better, and sank at the improbability of her promise.

Chapter Eighteen

Elisa hung up with Mom as soon as they turned onto Birch Street. She sighed and pressed her head against the seat.

"Everything okay?"

"Not really. My dad is having a tough time. Missing my brother. Easter can't come quick enough—I just can't wait to see them." Elisa squinted at the budding trees passing by. "I wish that my memories as a little girl weren't mixed with the constant gloom of my father's disappointment. I guess I understand why you are so protective of Blythe. There's nothing worse than watching someone you love lose heart because of another." She fiddled with the door handle. "All this goes to show that life's too short. Charlie never made amends with Dad…and my poor father has to live with the repercussions."

Sean pulled into the driveway and parked the

truck. "I am sorry, Elisa. I can't imagine a father losing a kid—my dad was beside himself when Blythe gave us that scare." He stared just past Elisa, lost in thought. She recalled Marge saying how hard he was on himself. Sean Peters didn't see what Elisa saw in him—what the whole town saw in Howard's son.

Elisa dipped her head in his line of sight. "Thanks for the coffee. It really helped." She hadn't planned on sharing her devastation with Sean today. But processing her grief aloud had been surprisingly therapeutic, especially since Sean understood the strife of tough relationships.

"Good. I am glad."

"Sean, I… I just want you to know how much I appreciate all you've done for me." She searched his eyes now that she had his full attention. "Like I told Marge, I… I have never met anyone like you."

The corner of his mouth quirked up, and his eyes danced along her gaze. "You told her that?"

Elisa blushed. "Not exactly. I mean, you're just so compassionate and kind. You don't know how much you mean to me—" Did that just come out of her mouth? Maybe it was the fog of the headache messing with her clarity. Her widening eyes only mirrored Sean's, until he glanced down at her lips. But unlike that first time they'd found themselves in this awkward interaction,

Elisa didn't feel so horrified. Sean Peters *did* mean something to her. His presence was a soft place to land here, in Rapid Falls, when life was hard—whether it be from growing pains with parenting or devastating reality checks about old relationships. Elisa dropped her gaze to his lips, too, and leaned in. His breath was warm against her skin, and his hand lifted to her cheek.

"Elisa—" He moved backward, not toward her. "We can't do this."

"Yes, you are right." She had just sabotaged a morning of work because of the last relationship that had crashed and burned. Obviously, her headache had obliterated her good reason.

She scooted back, embarrassment flooding her from all corners of the cab. Last time she'd felt this humiliated, she'd sat in the back of a vintage car, with a driver barely looking at her through the rearview mirror. Now Sean sat across from her, barely looking at her, too.

"There is too much at stake, don't you think?" Sean rested his elbow on the steering wheel. "I mean, you have become really important in my life—" He fluttered his eyes shut. "We're both trying to make our professional life work while caring for the girls. It's a lot—and I don't trust—" He exchanged his glasses for his sunglasses. "I just think we shouldn't do anything we'll regret."

"I am sorry, Sean. I got carried away." She breathed in every last particle of coffee aroma mixed with Sean's spicy scent. "We aren't in a place to trust our hearts, right?" She laughed and rolled her eyes, hoping whatever redness in her fiery face was fading lightning-fast.

Sean smiled and reached for his door handle. "Let's meet at the gate in about half an hour? I can't wait to show the girls the playset."

"Sounds good."

Elisa exited the truck. Sean took the side gate to the back while Elisa went through the opened garage door, trying to walk off her humiliation. Distant crying grew louder as she opened the kitchen door.

"Hello?" She followed the whimpering to the living room.

All three girls were on the couch—Ava was curled up in a ball, asleep, and Lottie sat on Blythe's lap, tears streaming down her face.

Blythe glanced over at Elisa. "Look, Lottie. She's back."

Lottie sprang off the couch and ran to Elisa, wrapping her arms so tight around Elisa's legs that Elisa worried she'd fall backward.

"Hey, there. Why are you so upset?"

"You left us!" The little girl began to cry forcefully, her chest skipping with breaths.

Blythe stood and swiped some moistened hair

from sleeping Ava's tearstained cheek. "They saw you and Sean leave in the truck." Blythe raised her shoulders. Her eyes bulged in bewilderment. "They've been crying on and off ever since."

Elisa crouched down and wrapped Lottie in a hug. "That's a long time to be upset. Lottie, you are at preschool for much longer than we were gone."

Lottie's little arms were stiff and tight around Elisa's neck. "But you didn't say goodbye," she whispered, hot breath on Elisa's skin.

"Oh, I am sorry." Elisa picked up the little girl and went to the couch to sit down. Ava woke up and scrambled over to Elisa. "Girls, I am right here, no worries." She smoothed Ava's curls and gave Lottie a kiss on the forehead. Blythe began to pick up some toys strewed across the living room. Elisa couldn't budge because the girls were attached to her with extraordinary strength. She spied Sean outside, inspecting the almost finished play structure. "Mr. Sean said the playset is almost ready. Want to go see it?"

The girls nodded. Elisa's phone dinged with a text. She pulled her phone out from her back pocket, Ava leaning heavily on her arm. The text was from Gerard.

We need to be at the client's house in Des Moines at noon tomorrow. Still planning on it?

Elisa sighed. She was hoping to work longer hours this week since Blythe was available all day. But the girls' separation anxiety was a little unnerving. Each day loomed ahead with the possibility of distraught nieces and exhausting commutes filled with worry. Elisa sank into the couch and cuddled the girls, craving another latte and an impromptu business meeting with Sean, fighting the urge to say no to Gerard. If only interior designers could be on spring break, too.

Elisa texted Gerard back with the expected Yes, then another text popped up. From Sean.

Ready when you are.

"Mr. Sean's waiting for us, girls." Lottie and Ava released Elisa and ran to the four-season room. "We've got to go through the garage, remember?" Blythe took their hands and they all hurried through the house.

Sean met them and opened the gate. "Spring break has now officially begun."

"It has a swirly slide." Lottie squealed as she ran between the orange fencing.

"Be careful, there are a couple of steps up to the terrace," Sean called out, but Blythe was a good helper and guided each girl carefully.

Elisa laughed when she saw the joy on Lottie's face as she slid down the slide. Blythe was at the top, situating Ava in her lap.

"It's amazing how quickly they go from tears to thrills," Elisa blurted, uneasy about any weirdness from the truck incident. But Sean was only staring at his phone. Glowering, really.

"Hey, are you okay?"

"Tears and thrills, yes. Blythe texted earlier." He didn't look her way, just kept his eyes on his phone, his jaw working. "Um, sorry, I didn't see Blythe's text until we were already back." He tilted his head up with a sharp intake of air, then stuffed his phone in his pocket.

Elisa would never pry, although a tweak of worry set in her designer brain. Were there any hiccups with this project?

She became acutely aware of Sean's mannerisms while the girls broke in the playset—the way he stared off when Blythe and Elisa were chatting as they pushed the girls on the swings, and the quick check of his phone when he'd stayed behind as the girls skittered along the bouncy bridge.

Elisa's phone vibrated with a reminder for an afternoon meeting. She called out to Blythe, who was helping Lottie climb up a ladder on one end, "Blythe, I am going to go work a bit. Girls, I'll just be inside."

Lottie thrust her head back and yelled, "Okay!" Ava mimicked her sister.

Sean joined Elisa down the path back toward the house. "That should keep them busy for a while." Again, Sean checked his phone, a crinkle appearing above the rim of his glasses. "I… I just can't believe this," he muttered to himself.

"We're on track for the flagstone install, I hope." Elisa was weary of the four-season room being off-limits for so long. "I would really like that to be next, if possible."

"What? Oh, no, not that." Sean glanced back at the girls. He lowered his voice. "Mom keeps texting. She's…she's not doing well."

"Oh, I'm sorry. Is it career-related?"

"Career?" Sean grimaced. "That ended a while ago."

"Oh, Blythe and the girls watch her videos."

"It's probably the same one over and over again." Sean sighed. "Mom's sick. Has been for a long time. Blythe doesn't know. She idolizes the woman, and I don't have the heart to tell her."

"Is it something she'll recover from?"

Sean shrugged his shoulders. "It all depends on how well she takes care of herself. She's been struggling with early onset chronic obstructive pulmonary disease. She hasn't coped well when it worsens, and she is not comfortable living alone anymore." He pursed his lips, then let out an exasperated sigh. "She's trying to get into an assisted-living home."

Elisa folded her arms across her chest, resisting the urge to reach out to Sean. She didn't want Blythe to wonder what they were talking about. "That's a big secret to keep from your sister."

Sean's face stiffened like stone. "I know it is. But she'll want to go over there and see Mom. She already wants to. And we just can't afford it right now."

"What about moving her here?"

Sean just wagged his head as if Elisa didn't understand. He strode ahead and slipped back into the construction zone.

But really, she did understand. No matter what happened in the past, Elisa knew the grief of withholding a relationship until it was too late. Her dad suffered because of Charlie's resistance. Elisa also regretted not knowing her brother like she should have. It had taken her work conference to Austin to finally realize how much she'd missed. A little too late. Or just in time, she guessed, since he entrusted her with his daughters in his will sometime between her visit and the accident.

Elisa glanced over at Blythe, then back at Sean. She also understood the feeling of being in the dark for so long, that when light was shed on the situation, heartbreak was inevitable.

What good was Sean's protection if it kept Blythe in the dark about the one person she hoped to reunite with one day?

Sean shouldn't have said anything to Elisa about their mom. But Mom was asking him for more money. He'd followed in Dad's footsteps and wired her money six months ago, against his better judgment. She'd chosen to leave, so why did they have to help her financially? He was finally figuring out a lucrative way to expand the business, and he wanted to hold off on spending until they had a couple more jobs in the books.

His conversation with Marge poked at his conscience. What if Mom was reaching out for more than money but in the hope of smoothing over the mess she'd made? And even if her mistakes had affected them all, Sean couldn't be so heartless as to withhold money from a woman with health complications.

Before meeting with the flooring guy, he texted her back and asked if she could send a bill for whatever treatment she referred to. His gaze shifted upward. Elisa stood at an upstairs window, watching the girls play. His heart twisted at her surprise that he'd kept Mom's condition from Blythe.

Sean wasn't so callous as to think he was doing the right thing by keeping it from Blythe.

He was just trying to protect his sister from the pain of Mom's dire situation. Even if Blythe did save money to fly to Hawaii, he wondered what Mom's health situation would be at that point.

On the way home, Sean stopped by a couple of clients to check on their flower beds. The Rapid Falls Retirement Center was one of Sean's favorite projects. He'd used the existing grounds as a model for one of his final projects in college.

The center had a courtyard in the back, flanked by three gardens—a vegetable garden supplying fresh produce for the center's kitchen, a prayer garden off the chapel doors, and a sensory garden, often a destination for school field trips, an added delight for the center's residents. After today's roller coaster of emotions, Sean took his time in the prayer garden. Nobody was around. He knelt beside the pond and weeded, but mostly, he prayed. He prayed for good financial decisions and that the business would thrive. Was that really the greatest need he should pray for?

His fingers yanked at a stubborn weed, but the roots hung tight to the earth, only the leaves breaking in his hand. He pulled out a trowel from his toolbox and began to work around the root to dislodge it from the earth.

"Hey, there, Sean." Edward Shaw, the center's new nurse practitioner, crossed from the archway to the lawn. "Wasn't expecting anyone to be here."

"Ah, I was just checking on the new plantings. And getting rid of these little impostors." He chuckled as he continued to dig. "How's the new job going? Shouldn't you be heading home about now?"

"I am between shifts." Edward sat on a bench across from the pond and opened a lunch box. "As for the job, it's been great getting to know our wiser residents." He grinned. "Mostly, I am thankful for the way the center partners with loved ones to make this place truly feel like home."

Sean breathed in the scent of fresh blooms and cut grass. "I know my grandmother loved it here. Wish she could have enjoyed these gardens."

"This one is my favorite." Ed began to unwrap a sandwich. "It's a nice place to contemplate— especially when a patient has had a tough go… like today."

Sean offered a commiserating smile. He first met Edward when he worked at the clinic where Dad received treatments. Sean had appreciated Edward's sympathetic care then. Sean sat back on the path and hooked his arms on his knees. "Seems I find myself here for a similar reason."

"Oh?"

Sean wasn't about to make the same mistake

twice by letting someone in on the complications with his mom. "Just a family member needing help. I am spread a little thin right now."

"Heard you're taking on a big project at the old Victorian?"

"Yes, sir. Hoping to spur more business that way." Sean twirled the trowel.

"Your dad would be proud." Edward leaned forward, resting his elbows on his knees. "He was one of my favorite patients." He glanced through the archway. "Is there anything I can do to help with your...family member?"

"Nah—" Sean's chest constricted. If only Mom hadn't run off to the farthest point in the United States. Edward *could* help her. "Just pray that I have some wisdom in all of this."

"Will do. And pray for Hal Kerr. Can't give details. But prayer is essential right now."

Sean nodded in affirmation. He went back to the weed, worked the trowel some more and yanked it out, leaving more room for the health of the ornamental plants to grow.

Sean prayed one more prayer. *Lord, weed out the resentment in my heart to make room for whatever You have in store.*

He packed up his toolbox, said good-night to Edward and headed home.

Chapter Nineteen

The rest of the week went by in a blur for Elisa. The girls had a hard time when she'd leave in the morning. Blythe was good at distracting them, promising dance-offs and singing. Knowing that Sean withheld their mother's condition from his sister only added to Elisa's fervor to pray on the drive to work—for her nieces' peace and for provision in Sean's and Blythe's lives as well.

At work, Elisa was elbow-deep in design revisions for her much too high-maintenance client. She didn't have time to think of anything beyond material samples and reworked plans. The two mornings she stopped by Sally's boutique seemed to boost her energy for longer days ahead, but when Friday evening came by, Elisa entered the house with her shoes hanging from her fingers and her body tense with worry about unhappy children. But the house was unusually quiet. Come to think of it, the girls hadn't run out on the porch, half crying and half laughing with relief from her return, like they had before.

"Hello?" She tossed her heels in the mudroom and walked to the living room. The house was tidy. Blythe was a good sitter in more ways than one. Maybe they were on the playset. She turned to go back out the garage, but she stopped mid-pivot. The gray of dusk outside was faded beyond newly installed landscape lighting.

Excitement filled her chest. "Wow!" she exclaimed as she stepped into the four-season room, now refinished with the flagstone that continued all the way beyond opened folding glass doors into the patio. Recessed lights illuminated the steps down from the room to the patio, a seamless transition.

Elisa hadn't expected such refinement this early in the project. The rest of the backyard wasn't finished, but this transition space was complete. And it was exactly how she had envisioned it.

"What do you think?" Sean stepped down new stone steps from the upper terrace. "We still have a bunch to do, but you said this space was priority, so…" He held out his hands, glanced around the patio, then set a satisfied gaze in her direction.

"Sean, it's perfect." She rushed up to him with her arms out, then stopped herself. This was a project, not a gift of endearment. "Exactly what Innovations wanted." She blushed, dropping her hands to her side.

"I'll take a hug." His hazel eyes gleamed from behind his spectacles. And that dimple appeared in full force, luring her into the arms of this amazing man.

His embrace was strong but gentle, as if he wasn't only hugging his friend but something precious, something to be savored. Her cheek pressed against his warm shoulder. How long had it been since she was sincerely hugged by a man other than her father? And even though she'd known Sean for only a couple of months, he had grown to be her closest friend here in Rapid Falls—he'd become this person who felt like…like the perfect accompaniment for a comforting night spent in peace and quiet, and maybe with a good book. She pulled away and searched his familiar features. Not a good book—more like good conversation. A safe place to speak about things of the heart and receive support. A sounding board for her needs, and they weren't ridiculous, but completely satisfied by a compassionate friend. How could one person encapsulate Elisa's feeling of contentedness?

"Hey, there," he muttered, slipping his hands from her shoulders to her hands. "That was one of the best hugs ever."

"You took the words right out of my—"

"Auntie!" The girls raced down the construction path, Blythe following after them. Lottie stopped and peered through the orange netting. "We can put our toys back in our room now!"

Elisa snickered at that. "Not likely, Lottie." She stepped away from Sean, reframed her thoughts back to business mode and said, "We will definitely wait for the toy explosion *after* the tour."

Sean chuckled, but after his laughter faded, his smile remained, and his eyes glowed with something that Elisa could only describe as hope.

Her business mind and her girlish heart warred against each other. Of course, this completed project phase was a triumph for a struggling landscape architect. Regardless of reason, Elisa couldn't help but wonder if his hope had something to do with her. That hug really was one of the best.

All Elisa's exhaustion from the week seemed to flit away with the golden light, the seamless transition space and that hug.

Elisa, Blythe and the girls went inside while Sean cleaned up some tools in the backyard. "How about pizza, girls?" She pulled out her phone to order as she plopped on the couch between Lottie and Ava while Blythe gathered up her homework and backpack.

"I got an owie." Lottie held up her finger as she nestled against Elisa.

Blythe explained, "It wasn't too bad. Nothing that a Band-Aid and a little entertainment therapy couldn't help." She strolled into the living room with her backpack on one shoulder, glancing out the dusk-dimmed windows. "I might just go out back to see if Sean's ready—"

"I wanna see the lou-lou again." Lottie stood on the couch cushion and reached over Elisa's head for Blythe.

Promptly, Elisa caught her by the waist and sat her down playfully. "Lottie, you are going to topple right off this couch and get a bigger cut on your head."

"It's not a cut. It's an owie."

"I assumed since there was a Band-Aid involved—" Elisa turned to Blythe.

Blythe shrugged her shoulders. "It's a cut. Owie sounds more…important, I suppose." She grinned wide.

"Ah, I see." The preschooler jargon was still not fully integrated into Elisa's vocabulary, it seemed.

"Lou-lou!" This time, Lottie sprawled across Elisa's lap, reaching her hands for Blythe.

"What are you talking about?" Elisa lifted her phone in the air to avoid it being knocked to the ground.

Blythe sat on the couch next to Ava, tucked her backpack between her feet, then gathered the two-year-old into her lap. The young teen held her phone screen out for all to see. "Lottie means luau. It's a video of my mom. Seems to help soothe her owies." She winked at Lottie, who giggled. "Mine, too," she mumbled as she swiped her screen and pressed Play.

A woman in a sequined dress and a bright pink lei stood on a dark stage, the spotlight as golden as the lights on the patio.

"That's Blythie's mom!" Lottie exclaimed. Blythe's smile only grew, and she watched the lively performance as if it was the first time she'd seen it—completely engaged. Ava and Lottie both wiggled to the beat. Sean appeared in the four-season room. He stopped in his tracks, dropped his gaze and leaned against the doorjamb.

When the song was over, Blythe sighed and tucked the phone in the pocket of her backpack. "One day, I'll make enough babysitting money to go to Hawaii myself." She nuzzled Ava's cheek with her nose.

Ava squealed and wormed her way to the floor.

"Ready, Blythe?" Sean cleared his throat.

Blythe sprang from her seat. "Yep. Let's get pizza, too, Sean." Her brother nodded.

Elisa scooted to the edge of her seat.

"Don't get up, Elisa. We'll see ourselves out." Sean crossed over to the front door, squeezing his sister's shoulder as she joined him. Ava and Lottie ran up behind the siblings, prattling on about Blythe staying longer.

Elisa turned around, leaning over the back of the couch as everyone else swarmed the foyer. "Girls, you'll see Blythe Monday afternoon." A deflated groan erupted in unison from the two sisters. Sean flashed a sumptuous smile that dissolved whatever tension had hardened his features during the chorus of his mother's performance.

Elisa's stomach flipped, and that creeping contentedness brought on by Sean Peters gripped her with full force. "Do you all want to have pizza with us?" Her spontaneous words came out on a high, cracking voice. She cleared her throat and said in a normal tone, "I mean, if we're both ordering, anyway—I can provide the paper plates."

Blythe nodded quickly and cast a pleading look at her brother.

"Sure, that would be great," Sean agreed. The little girls jumped up and down, Blythe set her backpack down, and they bounded upstairs upon Lottie's request for Blythe to build a fort in her bedroom.

Sean placed his toolbox by the front door while Elisa scrolled through her phone for the pizza place again. Suddenly, that contentedness she'd savored disappeared as quickly as the girls. She was with Sean Peters, on a Friday night, and the only decisions to be made had to do with pizza toppings and conversation starters. Easy. Then why did he look so uncomfortable, rocking on his heels with his hands in his pockets?

Witnessing Elisa's elation when she walked out to the patio earlier was the greatest compliment a guy could receive—a landscape architect guy, of course. Sean had never expected such a reaction from a high-end designer like Elisa Hartley.

But why not?

He'd gotten to know her pretty well these past few weeks. And in that time, she'd transformed from the stranger holding back tears in the back seat of his dad's old convertible Mustang to an amazing, perfect fit in his arms, if that hug indicated anything at all. How had Chad let her go? There was nowhere else Sean Peters wanted to be but in this cozy living room, ordering pizza on a Friday night with Elisa.

Had he ever had such a laid-back night with Kylie?

Ugh. Of course, they'd had nights at home. So

many small-town nights at home that Kylie had taken off out of sheer boredom, never to return.

"So, what's the plan?" Elisa asked as she held the phone to her ear. Plan? All he could think about was Elisa's uncertainty to stay here—her plan B. There was no use allowing his revved emotions to lead his heart into complicated territory. He had bigger things to worry about—like managing Blythe's expectations about Mom. His conscience had broken him in two when he saw Blythe so mesmerized by that old video.

"Plan? I… I—" What was the plan for his growing feelings for this woman leaning against her couch, barefoot, in a pencil skirt and nibbling on her lip as she waited for his reply?

"Two pizzas? What do you think?" Elisa turned her attention to the phone call. She arched her eyebrow his way. "How about one cheese, one supreme?"

He gave a thumbs-up, pushed his glasses up and decided to take his cue from the squeals from upstairs to stop thinking so much and enjoy the evening.

When Elisa hung up, she insisted they grab some drinks and head to the four-season room. "I would love your opinion on furniture." She sipped her iced tea.

"Work talk on a Friday night?" Sean quirked his eyebrow.

Elisa sighed. "I can't help it—this is such a great space."

Sean walked outside and jogged down the steps. He swiveled on his heel and looked up into the night sky. "I wonder if you'd want to go with no furniture at all? Keeping it cleared for a stargazing blanket would be best." He squinted. "We might need to kill the lighting, though."

"Not the lights! I love them." Elisa joined him, following his upward gaze. "They'll have their competition, though." Nightfall was just settling in, and stars had made their appearance. She returned to the steps and sat down facing the backyard in its entirety. "I'm going to have our firm's photographer get some initial shots. I'm sure he'll give you raw images for your own marketing use."

"Thanks, Elisa, that would be great." He sat down next to her, swirling the ice in his glass. "How's it coming with Sally's boutique?"

"It's been delightful. She's actually going to pay me for some drawings. She's got a contractor in mind already."

"That's great."

"Sally's so much easier to work with than my client. And my boss, if I'm honest. I think half my stress is from his barking orders...at me." She set her glass on the brown-and-gold flagstone. "There's something to be said for owning your own business," Sean said. "Have you thought about it?"

Elisa pushed her head back and looked at him straight on. "Among caring for two little girls, a remodel and juggling existing projects?" A hint of sarcasm narrowed her eyes, then her face collapsed into a grin of surrender. "Not likely."

"It's not easy, but I love working for myself." He hesitated. "Well, I loved working with my dad. But owning the biz is a close second."

Music floated down from the upstairs window, and his mom's singing began, landing like leaden wings on his shoulders.

"You know, Blythe is a pretty strong kid." Elisa spoke low, seemingly with caution. Why had he mentioned his mom's situation earlier this week? His usual protective walls were wearing thin as he grew acquainted with Elisa.

"I know she is. I just—I don't want her to get disappointed. Imagine if you thought someone you cared about turned out to be something they aren't—"

Elisa leaned on her elbow, straightening her head as she leveled her eyes with his. "Uh, I kinda know how that goes, yes." She softly laughed. "It's tough when our dreams depend on another person to fulfill them."

She was talking about Chad. And she had no idea that Sean kind of fit that description—

minus the "*someone you cared about*." She only cared for the escape driver on her wedding day because he'd saved her from facing a church full of guests. He stole a look at her now. She wasn't dipping her head in sorrow like she had about Chad's engagement. No, her umber eyes were round, unassuming, waiting for Sean to speak.

"The last time Mom came to Rapid Falls, Dad had been adamant that he wouldn't get a divorce. He said there was no reason. And actually, Mom agreed. Said she didn't care about any other man. But she just couldn't give up her dream. We were not her dream. So, what did Dad think? He had married a woman who set aside being his wife, and mother of his kids. Someone he cared about didn't care enough to stay." Exactly what happened with Kylie and Sean.

"That's big of your dad—to let her go and allow her to return."

"I think he thought she'd eventually realize what she was missing. Each time she visited, she left again. He never learned his lesson." Sean pursed his lips, trying to keep the emotion at bay. His father's last days had been hard. Why had he asked about Mom during the end—after all that had happened? "I offered to pay for Mom's ticket to his funeral. She couldn't come."

"A show?" Empathetic exasperation softened Elisa's features.

"No, she was ill. That's when I found out she wasn't performing anymore."

"And she doesn't want to come here now?"

"I don't really know. But she's asking for money I can hardly provide. Don't know how we would afford to move her." As much as Sean wanted to be Blythe's knight in shining armor, his insides twisted with the thought of facing his very first heartbreak, day in and day out— his own mother.

Elisa was quiet, fiddling with the hem of her skirt.

"I am sure you are thrilled you invited me for your Friday night." Sean leaned in and bumped arms with her, desperate to alleviate the gloom. "Look, don't worry about us. Like you said, you have plenty on your plate. I just want to figure out a way to encourage you to stay." Whoa, did he just say that?

Elisa quickly looked over at him, searching his face, a coy smile on her lips. "Oh, really? Once this backyard is done, I really have nothing left for you, Mr. Peters."

Sean rubbed his hand on his jeans and tilted his head, trying to redeem all the ridiculous vulnerability he poured out tonight. "I know, but you and the girls are making your mark in Rapid Falls. Especially with my sister." He winked at her, as if she knew that he may be using his sister as the entire excuse—when in fact he would be affected by her plan B, too. When had Sean had the chance to chat with someone so candidly, besides dear Marge?

The doorbell rang.

"Pizza's here," Elisa blurted. Sean popped up and held out his hand to help her up. Her fingers grasped his palm, and he enclosed her hand. She didn't know it, but the first time he'd held her hand to help her, he was rushing her into the getaway car on her wedding day.

Could he have ever imagined that the runaway bride would end up living just down the street? Only this time, Sean would never provide the vehicle to take her away, because if there was one thing he wanted as much as peace about his mother and Blythe, it was Elisa Hartley staying in Rapid Falls.

Chapter Twenty

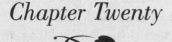

Elisa headed upstairs to get the girls while Sean took the pizzas to the kitchen. The ebony wood of the banister never failed to impress her with its smooth craftsmanship as she dragged her hand along it. This house had been an easy yes back in October, when she was presented with the opportunity to buy it. And while she loved the historical elements and the solid build, Elisa couldn't help but think that most of the reason she'd fallen in love with it was because she thought she had someone to share it with.

After the wedding, Chad had called and attempted an explanation and apology. All Elisa could focus on was getting this place on the market. Money had little to do with that decision. And the destroyed dream had most everything to do with it.

For the Peterses, it seemed that money had a

whole lot to do with alleviating pain. Her heart was heavy for their situation, and even for a man she'd never met—the late Howard Peters. They were on this side of a family-size destroyed dream. And while Sean was gallant enough to focus on protecting his sister, Elisa sensed that he suffered unresolved grief from his mother's decisions, even if he chalked it up to resentment only.

Before Elisa went into the bedroom, bracing herself for the complete chaos of Lottie's room turned into a bedsheet fortress, she pulled out her phone and checked her account.

The airfare credit for her never-to-be Hawaiian honeymoon just sat there with no reason to be used.

Until now maybe…

No. Sean Peters did not seem the type who would take such a huge gift. Elisa would have a hard time herself if the tables were turned. Wouldn't she? An ache groaned in her spirit. If it meant more time with Charlie before he passed away, then how could she not?

But this wasn't an alternate universe where a second chance at getting to know her brother existed, and it wasn't her place to meddle in someone else's family affairs. An offer like airfare credit worth thousands of dollars would be a huge way of meddling. And besides, the gift would mean she was stating her opinion on their family matter—that someone should fly to Hawaii or someone else should return to Rapid Falls.

Elisa quickly turned off her phone and crammed it in her pocket. Sean had said it best—she had a full plate…and so did he.

What was it he'd said after that?

That he was trying to figure out a way to encourage her to stay.

An uncontainable smile tugged the corners of her mouth, and a gazillion wings flapped in her hungry torso. Hunger. That was all. Pizza was calling her name.

She burst into the bedroom like any heroine ready to face the monster—but this one was facing a preschooler disaster zone.

"Pizza time!"

The girls crawled out from under the bedsheets strewed over the footboard and Lottie's dresser. Energetic Lottie and her happy babysitter passed Elisa as she leaned against the door.

Ava toddled behind them and yanked at the hem of Elisa's skirt. "Please." Then lifted her arms up to be held.

"Of course, sweet thing." Elisa held Ava against her hip and kissed her cheek. The two-year-old tucked her head against Elisa's neck. To think that a little over a year ago she'd just met her nieces for the first time. Ava was less than a year old, so she probably had no recollection of the aunt who ate fajitas with Ava's parents on the deck of their Austin bungalow.

Moments like these made Elisa realize that loving her nieces was an invaluable gift amid the uncertainty of this new parenting season. This role thrust her into a whole new level of existence, really. She followed Blythe, who took the stairs slowly behind Lottie. The four-year-old led with the same foot first at each step. An adorable childhood rhythm.

"You are doing great, Lottie," Blythe encouraged, and Elisa echoed the young teen.

When they circled around the kitchen table, Sean offered to lead them in grace. Lottie and Ava shouted "Amen" in unison.

Relaxed conversation about pizza favorites and the upcoming Easter egg hunt filled the kitchen. Elisa bit into the vegetable-laden slice while Blythe talked about the hundreds of Easter eggs to be filled, now sitting empty in Marge's living room.

"It's so fun to help. Marge always has yummy lemonade, and Lula brings braided butter cookies." Blythe bit her pizza, chewing with great enthusiasm. "It's a Rapid Falls tradition since Sean was little, right?"

Sean nodded. "Marge hosted back when the egg hunt was at the city park. The Hudsons recently volunteered the orchard grounds since the event's gotten so big. I'll take the eggs to the orchard the morning of the hunt. Hiding them is fun for grown-ups." He wiggled his eyebrows at Lottie, who giggled. His silly expression faded with a warm gaze in Elisa's direction. "Want to help hide eggs next weekend?"

"Sure. My parents will be in town. They can watch the girls so there's no peeking going on." She winked at Lottie.

"Grandma and Grandpa will be here?" Lottie asked.

Elisa nodded, and the little girl's face lit up with excitement. "I miss them."

"Me, too," Elisa agreed. "It's been a long couple of months without them here."

"Blythie, do you know my grandma and grandpa?" Lottie spoke with a bite in her mouth. Elisa tapped her own mouth to remind her of manners.

"No, I don't." Blythe laughed. "You're lucky to have grandparents, Lottie. Family visits are the best." She beamed, exchanging warm glances with her brother. He looked over at Elisa. An understanding passed between them. Elisa's heart burst with compassion for the very meaning of family and the loss they'd both felt and discussed—Sean's dad, the relationship with his mom, and Elisa's brother and sister-in-law.

Although, as they sat around the table tonight, Elisa couldn't help but think this felt like family, too. She looked back at Sean again. He shifted his eyes to his plate. What would this transition to Rapid Falls have been like without Sean Peters and his sister?

Elisa had always been careful to not expect much from others—cherishing her self-reliance above all else. The one time she let it slip was with Chad—a dire lapse in her judgment. However, allowing herself to depend on Sean these past weeks made her question that maybe it wasn't about judgment at all, but about relying on the wrong person.

When Chad failed to show up, she'd been saved from a whole bunch of embarrassment by that guy who had driven her away in what was meant to be her ride to the reception. She was ever thankful that the worst day of her life was salvaged with at least minimal humiliation in front of her whole hometown. Sure, she'd relive it every time she visited Grangewood in the following weeks, but the right person in the right place made a huge difference.

Elisa didn't dare look up again. She just focused on her pizza. She did her best to avoid distracting herself with the possibility that Sean Peters had a lot to do with everything right about this place and time in Rapid Falls.

* * *

When they got home, Blythe started upstairs to get ready for bed but paused when Sean's phone trilled. "Maybe I forgot something at the Hartleys'?"

Sean saw the 808 area code, which meant Hawaii. He cinched his lips together and shook his head quickly. "Nope. For me." He quickly escaped to the kitchen and answered. "Hello?"

"Sean? Have you looked at the bill?" Mom's raspy question ended in convulsions of coughing.

His compassion for this sickly woman shook against the protective wall he'd erected over the years. "Uh, no. I haven't been at my computer."

"I am sure you are busy."

"It's been quite a week." Sean cringed at his cold tone. But this person wasn't the mom who haunted his memories—the woman who sang at bedtime when he was little; the mother who'd meet him at the corner every day on his walk home from school. She'd changed as he'd grown older. What had happened for her to abandon him—and her little girl?

"My social worker is pressing me to go to an assisted-living facility here. It's expensive and—" She coughed some more.

Elisa's question about Mom returning to Rapid Falls seared his conscience. How could that even happen at this point? He needed more time to get financially secure.

But this was his mother. Family should be priority.

Was this woman really family anymore? She'd turned her back on him long ago. The old grief he'd stuffed deep down as a young boy began to billow in his chest.

She sighed. "The place doesn't have much space left. I don't know what I'm going to do."

Rapid Falls Retirement Center had plenty as far as Sean could tell. But having Mom nearby? He'd have never thought of it until his conversation with Elisa. Ten years ago, he would have done anything to bring his mother home. But now? How could he face her after all the heartache she'd caused?

"I'll look at the bill and email you back with what I can assist with."

Mom thanked him, they said goodbye, then he ended the call.

"Was that Mom?"

Sean spun around. Blythe stood at the door. He nodded.

Her face blanched. "Why…why didn't you let me speak with her?"

"Sorry, Blythe. She wasn't calling to chat. Just…she needs some money."

Her nose scrunched with confusion. "Money?"

The fierce need to protect his sister from learning about their mom's condition fought with the sobering truth about keeping secrets. Elisa may have had a good point, but she hadn't been here when Blythe suffered from Kylie's rejection. Sean couldn't risk his sister's mental health right now. Blythe was doing so well.

"She's just in a tight spot, Blythe." Sean grimaced. "She's ill."

Blythe hurried over to him. "How sick?"

"Don't worry. I am working on getting her some money for some treatments. She…she has trouble breathing."

"Oh no. That's not good for a singer." Blythe searched his eyes. "Do you think we should go to her?"

"That's not an option right now." He rubbed her arm. "I'll do my best to get her some money. We can call her on Easter." If she answered her phone. Her phone usually went to voice mail.

Blythe seemed satisfied. "I'll text her, too." She swiveled on her foot. "And pray that she texts me back."

Bile thickened Sean's throat. After Kylie left Rapid Falls, Blythe had gotten a phone of her own. When Blythe asked for Mom's number, Dad had spoken with Mom and persuaded her to not mention her health to their daughter. The few times Dad had checked Blythe's phone, Mom

had basically sounded like a broken record—
*Things are wonderful. Hawaii is beautiful. And
I am so glad you are well, B.* Mom never mentioned hardship, never asked Blythe questions.

It was all for the best, though.

Blythe was the sole fan of a woman who'd missed out on her kid all because of a botched singing career. Sean couldn't risk dumping all the helplessness he felt in this situation on his thirteen-year-old sister.

Chapter Twenty-One

Both mornings that weekend, Lottie woke up asking if Grandma and Grandpa had arrived. Her anticipation energized Elisa to clean the house and prepare for having guests—even though Mom said they probably couldn't get away until Thursday.

Monday morning, Elisa parked in the pre-school parking lot, bypassing the drop-off line once again. Ava was fine. Cozy in her pajamas with her blankie bundled in her lap.

But Lottie had tears streaming down her face. "I want to go to Grandma's."

"Lottie, they are coming here. Only three more days." Elisa hoped. Mom had mentioned that Dad's family medicine practice was short-staffed—including his partner, who was ill.

"That's forever." The four-year-old's shoulders bounced with tiny sobs. Elisa got out and opened Lottie's car door.

"Please, Lottie, I need to get ready for a big meeting today." Begging a four-year-old to co-operate didn't seem like the best parenting move. The pressure building in Elisa's chest was mo-ments away from pressing against her own eyeballs. Starting her day off with heightened emotion, knowing she'd eventually face strong emotion from her boss and client, sent Elisa into turtle mode—wishing for her own blanket fort, with Sean's headphones and a book without any sadness or anger or voices at all.

Somehow, through the tears, Lottie complied, climbed out of the car and walked with Elisa and Ava to the school doors.

"Good morning, ladies." Jane sailed over to them. "Elisa, I wanted to officially invite you to the board meeting on Thursday at seven. We'd love your guidance on moving forward with the remodel."

"Oh—" Elisa had known the ask was com-ing. Every time she'd come to the school, ideas flooded her mind on the drive home. So much po-tential here. "I'll see. My parents are coming to town, so—" They could watch the girls, depend-ing on when they arrived. Maybe it would work out. Elisa explained Lottie's pout to Jane, and Jane suggested they put a star on Thursday on the class calendar so Lottie's friends could help her count down. Lottie seemed satisfied with that.

The rest of the day, Ava cooperated while Elisa worked, as much as Elisa could hope for. The mute button on her computer became a dear friend during intense video meetings with her boss. Texts from Sally were happy distractions from the monster project.

When Elisa picked Lottie up from preschool, no tears were evident, and the girls babbled in the back seat. Good. Elisa would drop them off with Blythe, head to Sally's to look at samples of wallpaper, then work on her laptop at Sweet Lula's. The day was shaping up nicely.

They pulled into the driveway after preschool pickup. Elisa noticed that Blythe wasn't the only one standing on the porch.

Her parents flanked the front door, beaming and waving like they had on the day she graduated from the University of Iowa. Elisa whipped her head around—where was their car? She saw it parked across the street.

"Oh, wow, girls. I have a big surprise for you." Elisa's voice shook with excitement as she pulled past the front walkway and into the garage.

"Choc-o-it?" Ava's pronunciation of *chocolate* made Elisa smile every time.

This time, her smile was in full gear. She laughed. "No. Even better."

The girls were endless with their questions, begging and pleading for the surprise. She hurried them out of the car and garage and ushered them toward the front door.

Dad turned the corner with his roller bag, and Mom followed behind him. "My two princesses!" He crouched down and opened his arms.

Both Lottie and Ava froze, Ava turning back and clutching at Elisa. Not for long, because Lottie yelled, "Grandpa!" and ran to his arms, enticing Ava to do the same.

"I am so glad to see you." Elisa nearly ran to embrace her dad, too, warming as if a blanket swaddled her insides and gave her permission to completely relax.

"We've missed you so much." Mom rubbed Elisa's back. The little girls wedged their way between the two women. "And you all, too." Mom bent down and picked up Ava while Dad lifted Lottie.

"So, what happened with being short-staffed?" Elisa asked.

"Dad's partner had a friend offer to moonlight for them. And the temp agency came to the rescue for the support staff. We knew it might work out this way, but we didn't want to get your hopes up."

Blythe tilted her head to catch Elisa's eye.

"Oh, hey, this is Blythe, our sitter."

"We met. Blythe updated us on all the cute shenanigans of Lottie and Ava Hartley." Dad chuckled. Lottie cupped her hand over her mouth and giggled sheepishly.

"I sure did," Blythe said. "Um, I was going to take the girls over to Marge's for the Easter egg filling. Should we go?"

The girls began to protest, wanting to stay home.

"Blythe, why don't you take the afternoon off? The girls want to spend time with their grandparents."

Disappointment dulled her blue eyes, but she quickly plastered on a grin. "No worries. I get it." She turned toward Marge's house.

Elisa's elation sank a little. Blythe had been enthusiastic about the tradition at Marge's. "Once they get settled, maybe the girls and I can stop by?"

Blythe spun around with a genuine smile. "That would be awesome. They'll love it." She waved at the girls, then ran over to Marge's.

"She's a sweetheart," Mom remarked as they took their luggage up the porch steps while Elisa opened the front door.

"Blythe has been so helpful."

"We met her brother, too—" Mom followed Elisa into the house. "He's a nice guy." Mom stood her luggage at the bottom of the stairs, set Ava down and swiped her hand along the curve of the banister. She looked around. "This is so much prettier in person." She marveled at the crown molding and complimented the color scheme in the living room. "And Sean was right, your work here is amazing."

"He's so encouraging," Elisa managed to say, but her cheeks just burned.

"Have we met him before?" Dad asked. Lottie scrambled down and asked Grandma to look at her toys.

"Nope. He was the very first person I met here. Remember, I told you how he shoveled my driveway for me?" Through the window, Elisa spied him across the backyard, working in the shade of the evergreens. "We'll check out his work after a while."

Her parents were coaxed over to the girls' play area.

Elisa headed to the four-season room to open the folding glass doors so her parents could get the full effect of the seamless connection of outdoor and indoor spaces. She was perfectly content in this moment. The most important people to her were now in Rapid Falls. All the difficulties of this season were redeemed by the love that had entered her house upon her parents' arrival. But she couldn't deny that she'd had a foretaste of such a comforting feeling on Friday night. The feeling hit her straight in the heart as she paused between the four-season room and the patio, captured by Sean's smile, now directly shining her way.

* * *

Sean waved his hand in her direction. Elisa smiled, her chin dipping and a blond strand falling across her face. She tucked it behind her ear and waved. How could such a casual greeting cause his heart to skip around his chest?

"Hey, Sean, when you get a minute, I want to show my parents the plans for the yard. Can you bring them here?"

"Sure thing," he replied, swallowing hard. Maybe he should walk over to her right now and tell her something he should have said the moment she first pulled up the driveway.

They had met before.

Elisa's dad had acknowledged Sean looked familiar when they met on the front porch. Sean had totally forgotten that before he rushed Elisa to the Mustang, her dad had thanked Sean for pulling the car around. Sean rubbed his jaw where his beard once was. It had assisted in this incognito gig the past couple months. If he hadn't kept such a ridiculous secret about his identity, Elisa's dad would know exactly who he was, and Elisa would, too.

Sean dragged his feet to get the plans from his truck. Maybe this wasn't a big deal? He'd just tell Elisa as soon as they had a chance to be alone. Upsetting Elisa was the last thing he wanted to do.

Sean opened the passenger door and pulled out the container of drawings from the back seat. His cell phone rang, and he answered it. The carpenter was calling about incorporating the Victorian garden structure with the pergola.

Elisa and her dad walked across the lawn while he was on the phone. She waved as they crossed the street in front of the truck, pulled out some Easter baskets from the trunk of a sedan, then seemed to wait for him as they chatted. Sean ended the call, pulled his sunglasses on and joined them with the drawing case tucked under his arm.

"Got the drawings, Elisa." He smiled and handed them to her free hand.

"Great. We're getting the baskets out while Mom entertains the girls." Her phone alarm went off. "Oh, I have to get on a phone call." She groaned. "Innovations is zapping all my energy."

"You're good enough to go out on your own, Elisa." Sean then explained to Mr. Hartley how many folks around town were interested in her work.

"Oh, really?" Dad hooked an eyebrow. "That's something to consider if you don't move back home."

Sean tensed. He wondered if they'd talked about her plan B recently, or if the option would be hanging in the air indefinitely. He yanked his baseball cap from his back pocket and crammed it on.

"Sean, are you sure you haven't been to Grangewood before? You are just so—" Mr. Hartley gasped. "You're the driver."

"Driver?" Elisa cast a confused look at her father. "He's a landscape architect, Dad."

Sean slid his sunglasses off and stuck them in his shirt pocket. He winced in Elisa's direction. "I used to have a beard. It was such a sensitive situation I didn't mention it."

"You didn't tell Elisa?" Mr. Hartley's surprise seemed to spark realization in Elisa.

"I… I meant to say something—"

"Driver?" Elisa paused, recognition dawning in her doe eyes. "You…you are the one who took me home…at my…" Elisa dropped the drawings case as her hand flew to her mouth.

Sean reached out and grabbed her shoulder. "When you didn't seem to recognize me, I couldn't figure out how to tell you—especially because you wanted a fresh start. I went to college with Chad. He knew my dad had that old car and wanted it for your…ride to the reception."

She wriggled away from him. "Sean, how could you keep that from me?"

"I was about to at Sweet Lula's, but it just seemed like water under the bridge. And I didn't want to upset you."

"But you knew from the very beginning who *I* was?"

"Chad had mentioned you were considering moving here—he never said you'd bought a house already."

Elisa grimaced, muttering, "Of course he didn't."

"That first night you pulled in, I wasn't sure if you didn't recognize me or if you just didn't want to talk about it." Sean stepped forward but Elisa stepped back. "I was just protecting you— giving you space away from that day."

"This…this is too much." She looked at her dad, who maneuvered himself slightly in front of Elisa, as if he were protecting his daughter. As he should. "Sean, you say the same thing about Blythe. Are you really protecting anyone, or just avoiding the truth?" Her disappointment obliterated his strength.

"My family's situation is different. That's something much bigger than a twenty-minute drive in a car." He regretted the words instantly. How insensitive could he be?

Elisa's color drained from her face. "You don't understand. The only person who saw my tears that day—was you. I don't just cry my eyes out any ol' time." He recalled her tears when she told him about Chad's engagement, and it seemed she did, too. Elisa dropped her gaze. "You and my parents. That's it."

"And it didn't affect my opinion of you then or now. In fact, Chad got a huge piece of my mind that night."

"Oh, great. That makes me feel better." The way she rolled her eyes signaled her sarcasm. "How can I know that someone I've grown to… to…" Fear flashed in her eyes, now bubbling with moisture. "How can I know that your help wasn't all in the name of pity?"

Sean couldn't stand seeing her upset like this. Her neck was red and blotchy, and her bottom lip quivered. "Elisa, not once have I done anything out of pity. Ever since you showed up in Rapid Falls, all I've been trying to do is—" The culmination of all his resistance finally broke the wall he'd built. "I've been trying to keep from falling in love with you."

He had been protective to a fault—his sister, Elisa, his heart. Trying to keep from getting hurt again had made him ignore the truth for far too long. This past month had given him more than purpose for his business, but he'd found hope because of this woman who'd moved in down the street. He may have built a space out back with finesse and sophistication. But he'd complicated everything by walling up the truth all this time.

Elisa only stared at him. Her soft brown eyes

round and searching his. Mr. Hartley slowly walked up to the house. Apart from the construction out back, silence hung between them.

Elisa whispered, "Sean, this isn't—"

He held up his hand, desperate to explain who he was apart from the mess he'd created. "Elisa. I've been hurt before. Really hurt. And maybe that's why I refrained from saying anything. I know how it hurts to be reminded of the pain. But no matter how much I tried to stop myself from feeling anything for you because of my past pain, the risk just seemed more and more worth it." He released a humorless laugh and ran his hands over his hair. Elisa opened her mouth to speak but he continued. He wasn't just being honest with Elisa. He was being honest with himself. "You're this stunning woman who loves design as much as me. The way you parent those girls—so tender and loving, and you've only just begun. I want you to be here for the long haul. I want to see you continue to grow into this amazing role as their guardian. I want to sit with you on a Friday night and debate over landscape lights or starlight. I just want to be with you. Not because I pity you."

Elisa swiped at her eyes, then picked up the drawing case and handed it to him. "Sean. I can't do this right now. I got away from a guy who kept things from me and who obviously didn't love me. He hid his true feelings from me, and I lost in the end." She turned and marched toward the house, her shoulders shaking.

Chapter Twenty-Two

Elisa took care not to slam the front door, although her frustration begged her to take it out on her fine, Craftsman-inspired masterpiece. Dad sat on the stairs, the basket dangling from his fingers.

"I am sorry, Elisa." Dad's blue eyes were the symbols of the comfort she'd depended on. In the past, when a storm had crossed his features, Elisa had worried the comfort might be stolen away. Charlie's treatment of Dad had caused Elisa's security to waver more than she cared to admit. "You never recognized him?"

She shook her head and fiddled with the basket in her hand. "I was a blubbering mess in the back seat of that car. I could barely see him in the rearview mirror. And he took me seriously when I said I didn't want to talk about it." Elisa leaned back on the door. How could the guy she'd begun to have feelings for be someone who made her feel so much like the girl left at the altar, gullible and betrayed?

Dad sighed. "He seemed like a nice guy back then, from what I could tell. Sounds like you all have grown close."

Through the glass doors of the four-season room, Sean appeared in the backyard. He pulled out his cell and shook his head. Maybe he'd received another text from his mother. Whatever it was, Elisa shouldn't know anything about the personal goings-on of her landscape architect.

She gathered in all the air she could muster and sat next to Dad on the stairs. "Once again, I was left in the dark by someone who I thought cared about me."

"Chad didn't have the guts to tell you how he felt. Sean seems different, though. Like he truly does care." Dad lifted his arm and wrapped it around her shoulder. Elisa leaned on her father. The one place she'd always call home—in her dad's arms.

"I just need to focus on what really matters. The girls. Sean Peters is just one more stressor in my life." She offered a weak smile, wiping residual tears from her cheeks. "I am so glad you and Mom are here. As soon as I saw you, I was reminded of what true family feels like." She leaned over and kissed Dad on the cheek. They rose and Elisa took both baskets to the pantry, noticing Sean had left the backyard again.

How had she not recognized him? He had those unforgettable hazel eyes—

He was wearing sunglasses that day. And she really hadn't focused on anything but the wedding she'd left behind.

The old feeling of wanting to rid herself of this place, like when she'd mourned her wedding-that-never-was, crept into her heart again. Living with Mom and Dad when they had first brought the girls to Iowa was difficult only because of the grief everyone suffered. But stress wasn't part of Elisa's pressure back then because her parents were pillars without question. She may have depended on Sean a little too much. He was not family. And now she could hardly imagine being in the same room with him without feeling like the fragile woman crying her eyes out.

Elisa joined Dad in the living room as Mom huffed down the stairs. "Those girls are full of energy. I'm surprised your ceiling hasn't come crashing down."

"As long as it holds up till the tour," Elisa mumbled. The tour was the reason she needed to be here at this point. All for Innovations…and Peters Landscaping. But what about the Hartleys?

Maybe she'd taken a detour to Rapid Falls to

reiterate that she should be more careful to trust others with her heart. How had a botched wedding not been enough of a warning?

"I hope that doesn't deter you from saying yes, Mom." Elisa boomeranged a hopeful look to each of her parents. "Can the girls and I still have your upstairs? I am thinking that putting this place on the market might be the best next step."

Sean tried to focus on work, but after the encounter with Elisa, and his mother texting him about a letter, he could hardly concentrate. Assigning a crew worker as overseer, he returned to his truck to search through his pile of mail. There was a letter addressed to him, with a return address from Honolulu.

Did he really want to read this?

After today's confrontation with Elisa and her father, Sean was depleted. He closed his eyes and leaned his head on the headrest.

Lord, give me strength for whatever is next. With or without Elisa or Mom. You've brought me this far.

When Sean opened his eyes again, he noticed Marge opening an upstairs window to the spring air. Marge had tried to be a pen pal with Mom and had mentioned Mom's remorse. Sean couldn't help but think about the strained relationship between Elisa's dad and his son. What if Mom was trying to make up for her mistakes? If Sean kept pushing her away, the loss might be unbearable in the end.

He traced the envelope's corner. After all the talk about keeping secrets and not being honest, Sean bolstered the courage to face the truth of the matter—his mother, reckless as she'd been with her commitment to her family, was hurting and in need.

Sean wished he had been honest with Elisa from the very beginning. The truth, no matter how difficult, was the only path to reconciliation.

As he opened the letter, he prayed for forgiveness for keeping all this from his sister, then he began to read.

Sean,
Thank you for being willing to send money. I know that I don't deserve it. I walked away when life became hard. Blamed it on my singing career. But I didn't trust myself anymore. Depression never let go of me after my mother died. And it caused me to strive for an unreachable goal. At the expense of my family. I learned that when Dad paid for counseling. But it was much too late to undo all that I had messed up. I've assumed you would never want to see me again, so

I haven't asked. But I want to come home.
Every time Blythe texts me, I long to see her.
See you. I miss Rapid Falls, too.
   Can you forgive me?
   Maybe I'll get well enough to visit. Just
praying the financial situation looks up for
all of us.
Love,
Mom

Tears welled in his eyes as he stared at his mother's handwriting. No matter how shaky it appeared, its familiarity consumed Sean's resentment like a wildfire. All the love a little boy had stuffed deep down in his heart finally broke through his walls. He hadn't only been protecting his sister and Elisa from pain; he had been protecting himself from feeling pain most of all.

He was willing to forgive Mom—or at least start the process.

Forgiveness was in and out of reach for Sean today. Who was he to withhold the very thing he longed for from Elisa, from the mother who'd finally admitted her mistake?

Sean wiped his eyes with his palms and drew in a breath. He couldn't return to work at this point: there was plenty of demolition happening in his chest, so he walked over to Marge's to see if Blythe wanted a ride home. There was so much left to say.

Sean tapped on the door and let himself into Marge's living room. Easter eggs were dotted all around the floor. A big bowl of candy was tucked between Blythe and nine-year-old Maelyn Hudson, the daughter of Lance Hudson, orchard owner and Sean's high school buddy.

"Hey, ladies, how's it going?"

"Good," Blythe replied.

Maelyn snapped an egg together and said, "Marge is upstairs with Amelia. She definitely needs a nap." She and Blythe exchanged looks and giggled.

"Maelyn's cousin is just a little grumpy. Marge is sitting for the Hudsons while they get ready for the weekend." Blythe tossed a filled egg in a large picnic basket. "Are Lottie and Ava coming over?"

Sean's back stiffened and he rolled his neck back and forth. "I don't think so."

Blythe's happy countenance fell. "Elisa said they would."

"Their grandparents are here. I was just coming to tell you I am heading home. Want a ride?"

"Nah, I'll walk. We have a lot to do still."

"Okay." Sean turned to go, thankful to have time to sort through everything that had happened today.

"Hey, wait." Blythe followed him onto the porch. "Could you go see if the girls could come over? Their grandparents can come, too. I mean, Lottie would love meeting Maelyn, and Amelia and Ava would have such a fun time together. It's something we've talked about—"

"Blythe. Stop. I am not going to beg them to spend time with you." His tone was harsher than he'd ever allowed it to be with his sister. He reached out to her, and she shifted away from his hand. "I'm sorry. I just had a bad day."

"Okay." She crossed her arms on her chest and stared at the deck boards. "I didn't want you to beg. They seemed to love spending time with me."

"Elisa and I got in a fight." He pulled out a chair from a wooden bistro table. "I was at her wedding in the fall but never told her."

Blythe scrunched her nose and joined him at the table. "That's weird. Why wouldn't you?"

"Because I didn't want to embarrass her, I guess." His sister pressed her chin up in a sympathetic gesture. "I regret not telling her, but I don't regret getting to know her. She's been through so much—like us. And she's reminded me of the importance of family. Her brother and Dad never had the chance to reconcile their differences."

"Like Mom and Dad?"

"Yeah. And me…and Mom. But I am wondering if that could change."

Blythe's lips parted as she searched Sean's face.

"Elisa brought up a good point about me. That even though my intention is good, I shouldn't keep the truth from people I care about. Especially you, Blythe."

"I really don't care that you went to her wedding, Sean." She rolled her eyes and giggled.

"No. About Mom."

Her face fell. "What do you mean?"

"She doesn't sing anymore, Blythe. Hasn't in a long time."

Blythe looked down at her finger, which was following the slats on the table. "I figured. When she does return my texts, she mentions not having worked in a while. That's why I thought I could help with marketing one day."

"Blythe, it's not that she can't find work. Mom's sick. She probably won't ever sing again."

"What? How do you know?"

"Dad had started sending her money for medical bills, and I've been trying to keep up with them now."

Blythe scooted back. "Is it really bad? We should go see her."

"That's the thing. It's so expensive to fly on

top of all the funds she needs. She requires full-time care, Blythe."

"She should come here." Blythe sprung up from her chair. "We'll take care of her."

"She needs constant care. Like Dad did." Sean stood and shoved his hands in his pockets.

"Please, Sean. We can help her." Blythe's bottom lip quivered. "I'll do everything I can. I am a good helper. Elisa says so all the time."

The old Victorian snagged his attention over Blythe's strawberry blond hair. The newest resident of Rapid Falls had made such a difference in his life. He should beg forgiveness from Elisa, but he feared it was too late. Their relationship was so new, so fragile.

He'd messed up big-time.

Mom's choices had made Sean overprotective in so many ways, and while his heart pulsed against a hedge of apprehension, the woman had asked for forgiveness at last. Maybe, just maybe, her coming home was a possibility?

Sean recalled his conversation with Edward Shaw. "I wonder about the retirement center. Maybe we could figure something out—"

"Are you serious?" Blythe's freckles were lost in a flush of red. She threw her arms around Sean and he couldn't tell if she was laughing or crying. Probably both. "I'll pray so hard for this to work. I'll have a mom again."

Sean squeezed her, his own tears threatening again.

Once Blythe went back inside Marge's, Sean crossed the lawn to his truck. He considered the time difference between Hawaii and Iowa and pulled out his phone. Mom should be up now. He texted:

Mom, I got your letter. What about Rapid Falls Retirement Center? Would you consider?

Before he crossed from Marge's property to Elisa's again, his phone dinged.

I would love nothing more.

Chapter Twenty-Three

The next morning, Elisa shared the schedule for preschool with her parents, and they all agreed to have Blythe watch the girls as usual. Elisa felt horrible that they never went to Marge's. Last night, she could hardly fall asleep as Blythe's disappointment clung to her thoughts. Well, that wasn't all she could think about. Sean's confession about his feelings for her warred with the hurt that he'd kept his identity hidden. However, she knew who Sean Peters was, and a driver on her most disastrous day was only a small role he had played in her life.

Or, one might say, he had been her knight in shining armor that day. Stealing her away in an old Mustang. The perfect steed.

Elisa drove to Marion, racking her memory of that car trip with Sean. But she kept bumping into the heartache of what Chad had done, and the embarrassment that followed her around Grangewood the following weeks. Could she ever disconnect Sean from that painful time in her life?

The day dragged on at Innovations. All Elisa wanted was for the day to end. She planned to call Sally and wrap up some loose ends for the remodel, then once she got home, she'd brainstorm ideas for the preschool board meeting on Thursday. If she was going to move away, she had so much to do before she left.

When she got home that night, her brain hurt from sorting through her feelings and her plans to leave Rapid Falls. But as she beelined to change into comfy clothes, Blythe practically tackled her in the living room. "You'll never believe this."

"What is it?" Elisa glanced around for Mom and Dad and saw them through the window. They were with Sean, examining the modernized Victorian structure at the very center of the yard.

Blythe gripped Elisa's arms. "Mom is moving to Rapid Falls! Can you believe it?" Blythe wrapped Elisa in a giant hug. "We're trying to figure out expenses."

"Really? That's…that's wonderful." She tried to tame her desire to run over to Sean and ask him how he was feeling about all of this. "Your brother's okay?"

"Sean said it was kind of because of you."

Elisa jerked back and searched Blythe for any indication that she was kidding. But the girl was being genuine, like Elisa expected from the Peters siblings. "I only asked him if he'd thought about her coming here. That's all."

"Yeah, but you also know how important family is." Blythe bit her lip. "And the girls losing their parents—your brother— We've all been through so much, huh?"

Elisa embraced her again. "We sure have. I am so glad you're getting your mom back, Blythe."

"Me, too. Can't wait for the girls to meet her. They'll have to sing for her."

"That's sweet." Elisa didn't have the heart to tell Blythe she was planning on selling the house.

"Now all we need to do is get the rest of the money for the move and the retirement center. Marge had a great idea to use the proceeds from her baked goods to at least pay for airfare. But Sean won't let her—the money is supposed to go to the women's shelter. He couldn't take that away from them."

"That's noble of him." An idea began forming in Elisa's mind. Finances were a huge obstacle for the Peterses, enough that Marge was bold enough to suggest fundraising.

Would airline credit from a secret donor be turned down?

Elisa steadied herself against the back of the

couch while Blythe ran upstairs to check on the girls. How could she explain why she would do Sean any favors at this point? She could convince any stranger, though, that it was for her sweet babysitter. But she knew that she wanted to help more than Blythe.

A question had poked at her the whole drive from Marion today: Was her season in Rapid Falls really over? What if finding out that Sean had been part of her wedding fiasco wasn't the end of her second chance, but a test of not only her loyalty to Rapid Falls, but her growing affection for Sean Peters?

While Elisa continued with her plan to tie up loose ends around Rapid Falls, her parents and Blythe entertained the girls, and Sean kept to his role as landscape architect and project manager. Every time she stopped at Sally's boutique, she resisted the onslaught of questions about her availability to take on projects for the knitting club's friends and relatives.

On Saturday morning, Elisa finally had the chance to step outside and take in the progress of the backyard without an awkward encounter with Sean. He'd mentioned hiding Easter eggs together, but that was before everything happened. She sighed and wrapped her cardigan against the crisp morning chill.

The backyard was beautiful. Pristine lines and well-appointed flower beds that would burst with color by the time of the tour. And the central feature—an exclusive Sean Peters pergola.

His debut into the design world was almost complete.

Dad met her in the four-season room. "Good morning, Lees. What a great concept for the garden structure, huh? We should eat under there for Easter lunch."

"That might be a tight squeeze."

"Mom's fixing the girls' hair and then we should be ready to head out."

"Sounds good. I am glad it's not too cold for the egg hunt this morning."

They went to the kitchen and filled up to-go coffee cups. She grabbed the Easter baskets, remembering the day they'd retrieved the baskets from Dad's car. When Sean had revealed who he really was.

"How did you recognize Sean, Dad? I mean, had you even talked with him at the wedding?"

"Oh, well—" Dad rubbed his chin and sat down at the kitchen table. "He was pretty unforgettable that day—considering the company."

Elisa joined him at the table. "What do you mean?"

"I was waiting for you to come out of the dressing room. Sean ran down the back pew and nearly tackled the best man in the narthex. When Sean relayed that Chad had sent a text that he wasn't coming, the best man was...well, downright crass. But Sean reprimanded him and was so concerned about—you...the bride. I'd never seen a stranger care so much about someone they didn't know."

"Sounds like Sean. Trying to take control," Elisa muttered. Dad raised an eyebrow. "In a good way."

Dad slowly nodded. "Sure. Control. Concern. It's telling what a man does when faced with something of such magnitude. Like I said, the best man was not so considerate. He cracked jokes about Chad's decision being a win for bachelors everywhere."

The best man was not someone Elisa cared to see again. He had been more about having a good time than being a friend. But Chad had often defended him—almost looked up to him in a way. Not surprising in the end.

Dad's profile was sharp against the bright four-season room in the background. Elisa focused on his chiseled nose, strong chin and steady lips. "While Sean ran out to get the car for you, Charlie approached the best man like any brother should."

"He did?"

"Yep. Nearly punched the guy." Dad's lips

twitched. She wasn't sure if he was going to smile or frown. "For that one moment, no matter how horrible that day had turned out for our family, I saw us as exactly that—a family. Including Charlie. A family who cared enough to protect each other at all costs." His Adam's apple bobbed, and he blinked several times as if trying to ward off his own tears. Elisa covered Dad's hand and sighed.

"This whole mess with Sean is because of his excuse to protect someone who isn't his family at all." Elisa inwardly winced, knowing how much the Peterses had felt like family in such a short time.

"Lees, you don't feel the same as he does?" Dad's poignant stare returned Elisa to her childhood when she would shove a beloved book beneath the covers well past her bedtime. He had known she was breaking the rules. And this time, even though he asked the question, Dad seemed to know the answer.

"I do. But I don't want to be blindsided again, Dad."

"I understand, honey. If there is one thing I've learned from Charlie's death, it's that God places people in our lives, with flaws and all. It's up to us to decide whether we extend grace or walk away." He pressed back in his chair. "I tried my hardest to overcome my divorce and its consequence of losing my son's acceptance. I never did receive his grace. But I tried my best to give it to him, even when he spoke the most hurtful things." He leaned forward and held Elisa's hand. "From what I can tell, Sean is one of the good guys."

Elisa knew that was true.

She'd seen this house as a retreat from all the hurt she'd suffered. But Elisa had never expected this place to open a door to a chance at love. While Chad had made her feel like she wasn't enough, Sean had told her he'd begun to fall in love with her—because of who she was. Until now, Elisa wasn't sure she believed it.

"We better get going." She gathered everything they needed for the morning at the orchard, including the envelope with the secret airline credit for the Peterses.

But after talking with her father, she decided keeping secrets had worn out their welcome in her home. She'd tell Sean about the credit. And it was time she was honest with herself.

She wasn't falling in love with Sean Peters. She'd already fallen.

The orchard was decorated with barrels of early spring flowers and rustic garlands of dried flowers tied with pastel-colored bows. Elisa assumed the entire town of Rapid Falls was either sitting on the orchard café's patio around pink-and-white checkered tablecloths or eagerly waiting elsewhere on the grounds.

"Elisa!" Marge approached with arms wide. "These must be your parents." Mom and Dad introduced themselves while Lottie and Ava eagerly accepted some candy that Marge dug out of her apron pocket. "Now, you all need to come inside and meet Lula. We are up to our bunny ears in selling baked goods." She giggled in her melodic way and started toward the café door. "Better hurry. We're selling fast."

"We'll be there soon." Elisa scanned the crowd. "Um, Marge? Have you seen Blythe—and Sean?"

Marge called over her shoulder, "They're passing out bags at the five-and-under area."

"I see Blythie!" Lottie pointed. The young teen stood beneath an archway of greenery with a sign that read Egg Hunt for the Littles. The sunshine brought out Blythe's strawberry highlights. When she saw Lottie and Ava, Blythe left her post and ran up for hugs, just as a red-headed woman stepped onto a small stage and spoke into a microphone.

"Welcome, Rapid Falls. It's a beautiful morning for an egg hunt." A girl with the same pretty hair color wrapped her arms around the woman's waist beneath her baby bump. The speaker continued, "I'm Piper Hudson and this is my daughter, Maelyn. Welcome to our orchard. This year, we have a special treat for you. Besides the regular eggs, a generous donor has donated several golden eggs—each with a monetary gift that will be matched with a donation to the Rapid Falls Retirement Center." The audience cheered and clapped.

Piper then handed the mic to Maelyn. "We will begin in five minutes." She smiled brightly and a cheer rippled through the crowd again.

Once the egg hunt began, Elisa tried to focus on following the girls and her parents around the egg-laden lawn, but she couldn't help but wonder where Sean was.

Finally, she walked over to Blythe. "Have you seen Sean?"

Blythe handed an egg to a child she was helping. "Sean went back into town. Said he needed to finish up some planting and wanted to get it done before Easter morning."

"Oh, I expected to see him out here."

"Nope, he's at your place."

Elisa spied her parents tending to the girls across the lawn, then turned her attention to Blythe again. "Do you think you could let my parents know that I will be back? I… I forgot something at home." She winked. "I am going to go pick him up."

* * *

Sean wanted to make Easter special for the Hartleys, even if Elisa was hardly speaking to him. Her parents had been so impressed with the pergola he'd decided to deck it out with garlands and flowers and hide a few eggs for Lottie and Ava.

He also planned to leave a note for Elisa. Asking for forgiveness and reiterating the one thing he knew to be true. He loved her.

When he turned around, he nearly stumbled back into the wooden post of the pergola. Elisa stood at the threshold of the four-season room and the flagstone patio.

"I assumed this would be the best place to meet you in the middle." She grinned and averted her eyes to the doorway above her, then the house behind her, and the patio between the two of them. "Even though the transition is pretty seamless." Her smile broadened, and she stepped into the sunshine. "Who knows where one room starts and the other begins."

He narrowed his eyes and crossed the expanse of flagstone. "True. But the process to get here was pretty messy." When they stopped, inches across from each other, he lifted his hand and swiped away a blond strand of hair from her cheek. "Beautiful, but messy just the same."

Her eyelashes curtsied with shyness, but then

fluttered open to a bright gaze. "Sean, I haven't been honest with you—or—me. This whole transition from abandoned bride to..." She searched his face. "To your friend..."

He pushed his glasses up and swallowed hard.

"I was so sure that Rapid Falls was this chance to hide away from all my hurt, but really, it was a place to heal." She stepped back and glanced about the yard. "The only part of these past two months that has been seamless is getting to know you."

"You did—you got to know the real me. I promise. I am sorry for keeping the secret about your wedding."

Elisa smiled, and her eyes sparkled. "Speaking of secrets, I was going to hide something from you." She closed the gap between them and placed her hand on his heart. Could she feel the stampede pounding in his chest, begging him to take her hand in his? "But I am tired of secrets, Sean." She pulled out an envelope. "This is for you. And I won't take no for an answer. They'll just go to waste because I plan on staying put in Rapid Falls for a very long time."

"You're staying? Here?"

She nodded but pushed the envelope toward him.

He opened it. Airline credit, in his name. Lots and lots of credit. "Are you serious?"

"Hey, I have to repay the knight in shining armor who drove me away from my most disastrous day." Her smile belied the word *disastrous*. Or maybe it didn't. Because Elisa Hartley's smile destroyed his composure, and he could only envelop her in a loving embrace with as much gentle strength as he could muster.

"Are you sure?" Their faces were so close together. He couldn't see anything but this beautiful woman who'd taken up residence not only in his town, but in his heart.

"About what, the credit?" Elisa scrunched her nose and smirked. "Without a doubt."

Sean narrowed his eyes and muttered, "How about us?"

"Well, a few days ago, I was ready to pack up and leave forever." She lifted up on her tiptoes and wrapped her arms around his neck. "Not anymore." Her lips pressed softly on his. "I love you, Sean Peters."

"You know I love you." He glanced at her lips without hesitation. And kissed her again.

When she pulled away, she tugged at his shirt. "Come on, we've got to go back to the egg hunt. I can't miss the girls' first Rapid Falls egg hunt completely." She took his hand and led him back toward the house. "Also, I am dying to take a ride in that Mustang, with the top down this time."

"Oh, really? It's at our warehouse."

"Let's go there first."

He chuckled, amazed that the bride he'd tried to help get away unexpectedly became the woman he would never let go. "Sounds like a plan."

And Sean Peters had finally found the missing piece of *his* perfect plan, no plan B needed.

Epilogue

Five months later

Elisa pulled into a space along Main Street and hurried out of her car. At least she'd arrived before nightfall. Today was incredibly important, for more reasons than closing the chapter on her high-stress job at Innovations. Her heart leaped at the sight of Sean and Lottie down by Sally's boutique, waving at her like it was a million years since they'd last seen her.

"Lottie! How was your first day as a kindergartner?" Elisa ran up, knelt down and gave her niece a big hug.

"It was the greatest day ever!"

"I'm so glad." She squeezed Lottie's hand.

Elisa stood, and Sean kissed her cheek. "And how was your last day as an employee, Miss Hartley?"

"It was a day—and now it's finally over." She glimpsed at the doorway. "The sign is finished!" Sean snagged her hand and Lottie held her other as she admired the windowpane.

Hartley-Peters Design Associates, read the elegant serif lettering.

"Should we go in and check out the final details?" Sean shook the keys.

"It's really ours, isn't it?" Elisa couldn't believe that she was a co-owner with the landscape architect of her dreams.

"It is. Sally was here earlier to see the remodeled space. She's so happy to have new tenants."

Sean tucked the keys in his pocket and opened the door.

"Couldn't wait until I got here to unlock it, huh?" Elisa teased. Sean smiled, holding the door open for her and Lottie.

They climbed the narrow stairs; the smell of fresh paint mixed with a familiar scent. "Was Sally just here? I smell her perfume—"

As Elisa reached the top stair, Sally and Marge stood together and said in unison, "Well, hello, neighbor." They both laughed.

"Sean didn't say you were still here, Sally. And Marge?" Elisa greeted her with a quick hug.

"Isn't this exciting?" Marge looked around. Elisa took in the final touches on the waiting area.

"Go on, Lottie," Sean whispered over Elisa's shoulder.

Elisa narrowed her eyes at Sean. "What's going on?"

Lottie giggled and opened Sean's office door. Ava toddled out first, then Blythe helped her mother through the doorway.

"I thought you all were taking Ava to the park?" Elisa exclaimed.

"Mr. Sean not let me go," Ava pouted.

"What? Why not?" Elisa spun around. Sean was down on one knee, with a crooked grin, and eyes filled with anticipation. Elisa could hardly speak, only managing to say, "Oh, Sean."

"Elisa Hartley, as if you didn't have enough on your plate—a new business and a business partner who falls more in love with you every day. But how about a wedding, too?" He pulled out a ring, his debonair smile competing with the twinkling diamond. "Will you marry me?"

Elisa laughed and cried and threw her arms around Sean Peters with a resounding "Yes," and her new family cheered all around her.

* * * * *

*If you liked this story from Angie Dicken,
check out her previous Love Inspired books:*

His Sweet Surprise
Once Upon a Farmhouse

Available now from Love Inspired!

*Find more great reads at
www.LoveInspired.com.*

Dear Reader,

This is my second story set in Rapid Falls. If you've read *His Sweet Surprise*, then you'll have recognized some characters. If not, then you will love that story, too!

When I first moved to Iowa, I had three small children. A reliable babysitter like Blythe was appreciated so my husband and I could go on date nights! We'd often stroll along our town's Main Street—the model for Main Street of Rapid Falls—and then return home to our three rambunctious little boys. The boys actually came up with the name *Rapid Falls*, when they'd make up songs while we drove between Cedar Falls and Cedar Rapids.

Besides those early years, I've also been inspired by women in my life, including my late Yiayia Lula (yes, sole inspiration for Sweet Lula's owner). Marge and her knitting club ladies represent the joy of friendship I treasure every day.

Stay tuned for details on my next Rapid Falls–based story by subscribing to my newsletter at angiedicken.com.

Sincerely,
Angie